COMPLETELY CASSIDY

STAR REPORTER

TAMSYN MURRAY

USBORNE

Tired of living a life you hate?

Of course you are. But did you know the power to change is inside each and every one of us? All you need to do is find a way to unlock that power! Start by writing it down here:

I TOTALLY need to spice up my life. I'm still looking for my thing – a talent that stops me being a Nobody and turns me into a Somebody. My theory is that everyone has something they do really, really well. Last term, I thought I might be an undiscovered genius but it turns out that's not my thing, so I'm stepping up my search. And if whatever it is turns out to make me really popular (especially with ~~Nathan Crossfield~~ You Know Who) and gets me some respect, I won't mind at all.

Also, I'd like the power to mute my brother, Liam, so that I don't have to listen to his moronic ramblings. And if it worked on my baby brother and sister too, that'd be AWESOME.

CHAPTER ONE

"Once upon a time there was a girl called Cassidy. She was gentle and kind, in spite of being poor and having a cruel older brother. Everyone loved her, especially her faithful dog, Rolo, and her besties, Molly and Shenice. She lived in a rose-covered cottage in the middle of the woods and every morning, she sang so sweetly that even the birds stopped to listen—"

WHAT IS THAT SMELL?

What **IS** it? Seriously, it is like something has died in my room. The twins are asleep in Mum and Dad's room – surely it can't be them? Then again, nothing would surprise me where Joshua and Ethel's bottoms are concerned. Having lived through some of their nappies in the last five months, I am amazed our house hasn't been declared a biological hazard. I know they can't help it but I am pretty sure I didn't do that when I was a baby.

I **SUPPOSE** it could always be Liam – he is almost fifteen and smells worse than our wheelie bin. But I think he is round at a mate's house and even he does not stink that much. Whatever the cause, it is making my eyes water. How am I supposed to turn my life into a fairy tale using less than five hundred words for double English tomorrow when the atmosphere around me is more poisonous than Saturn's? Some people might say it is my

8

own fault for leaving my homework until eight o'clock on a Sunday evening but that hardly helps me now, does it? There isn't even any way I can use the pong as an excuse for not doing my essay – ever since we came back after the Easter holidays, the teachers at St Jude's have been drumming into us that the end-of-year exams are just around the corner. Never mind that it is only the end of April and the exams are not until June – apparently, even physical evidence that the dog has eaten your homework is Not Good Enough.

Which brings me to the only other stinky suspect – my dog, Rolo. When I asked for a puppy for my tenth birthday, I didn't know we would somehow end up with one who was part chocolate Labrador, part T. rex. NOTHING is safe around him, as my dad found to his cost when he left one of his Elvis Presley wigs lying on the sofa and came down the next morning to find only the tufty black quiff left. And as the old saying goes, what goes in, must come out – pretty sure I don't need to draw you a picture. But as disgusting as Rolo is, he doesn't usually do his business in the house. And this smell is so bad, it can only be an inside job. I wonder if I can work it into my fairy tale somehow – CINDERSMELLA, maybe. Urgh. I will have to turn one of Mum's bras into a gas mask at this rate.

It's no good, I am going to have to investigate. Hey, maybe that could be my talent – I could be a great detective and solve crimes. One mystery...three suspects...a dangerous mission to uncover the truth...

Alright, it's not exactly Sherlock Holmes but even he had to start somewhere.

Mum and Dad were slumped on the sofa when I went downstairs. Mum was gently snoring and Dad was so engrossed in an ELVIS documentary that he hadn't noticed the smell.

"Although now you come to mention it, there is a hint of Brussels sprouts in the air," he said, wrinkling his nose. "Is Liam home?"

I shook my head. "It's either the babies or Rolo."

"Or both," Dad suggested, pulling a face. He glanced at Mum, who chose that moment to let out an especially unladylike snort. "Shall we investigate? I'll be Doctor Who and you can be my assistant."

"No, thanks," I said, following Dad up the stairs. "I'll be the Doctor and you can be the sidekick."

The stink that greeted us when we opened the door

11

was unbelievable. And we soon realized why – Joshua had had the kind of nappy malfunction they don't show you on the adverts. I'm not joking, his vest was basically an enormous brown stain, starting at his bottom and stretching all the way up to his neck. It looked like someone had spray-painted him while he slept.

Dad clamped his hand over his mouth. "Ah fink ee ave fan ver cubrit."

I pinched my nose. "Whad?"

He removed his hand and winced. "I said, I think we've found the culprit."

I couldn't argue with that – the evidence was pretty overwhelming. What I couldn't get over was the way that Ethel was sleeping soundly next to him, completely unaware that WORLD WAR POO had begun beside her.

Backing away from the horror, I left Dad to it and went to get the changing stuff.

Half an hour later the smell was STILL lingering, even though Dad had sorted Joshua out and opened a window to let some air in. I was back in my room and doing my best to concentrate on my homework, but the stink seemed to be getting worse.

After several hard sniffs, I decided that after all that the pong might actually be coming from under my bed, which kind of ruled out the twins. I thought about calling Dad again, but then I remembered that a good investigator does her own dirty work, so I took a deep breath and peered under the bed. And there, staring up at me, was a very embarrassed-looking Rolo. Holding a cushion over my nose, I leaned closer and saw he was encrusted from head to toe in something brown and smelly. The parts that weren't crusty seemed to be oozing. I have no idea what he'd rolled in – have the neighbours upgraded their tabby to a pet elephant or something? And it was just typical that he'd hidden in my room instead of Liam's. There's all kinds of rubbish and fluff under my bed, which probably explains why he had a Starburst wrapper stuck over one eye and – URGH – the pong! Let's just say it made Joshua's little accident seem like a walk in the rose gardens.

I have texted Molly and Shenice, letting them know that POOMAGEDDON has struck and that I might not survive the clean-up operation.

It's at times like this I wish we'd got a cat.

CHAPTER TWO

AAARGH! There is only one thing worse than being woken up at three-thirty in the morning by a screaming baby. And that's being woken up by two screaming babies. Especially when it's a school night and you've only just nodded off after the last time they broke the sound barrier.

Joshua and Ethel have the kind of cries that pierce pillows and it's turning us into sleep-deprived wrecks. Sometimes I think they wait until we've all drifted off

and then they attack, like tiny scratch-mittened ninjas.
Shenice says that sleep deprivation is an actual torture
method used by the CIA and I can totally
believe it; seriously, just brushing
my hair has become a task worthy
of THE CUBE and my eyes have
more bags than Asda. Molly
reckons that in the zombie
apocalypse, our
house will be
the safest
place in
Windsor,
because our brains
have already been
mushified by the
twins' supersonic
screaming. And if the
sleep deprivation doesn't
get us, the bad smells will.

My dad is being ridiculously cheerful about everything, despite the fact that he's up at four-thirty most mornings and actually fell asleep in his Weetabix today. Maybe that's why he's so keen to get to his deathly-dull day job — to get some rest. I don't expect anyone poos on him there, either.

"We have to try to enjoy them while they're little," he babbled this morning, cradling Joshua into his shoulder, unaware that a dribble of milky sick was trickling down the back of his shirt. "It won't be long before they're toddling around, causing chaos, and we'll wonder where the time went."

I tore a savage strip off my toast. I'd enjoy being a big sister a lot more if I didn't feel like my eyeballs had been pickled in nail varnish remover. Even Liam stopped shovelling cereal into his mouth long enough to give me a we're-in-this-together look. That's when I knew things were really bad; Liam really puts the UGH into ugly and we never agree on anything. Maybe the lack of sleep is dragging me down to his level.

Mum seems to have lost the power of speech. She just grunts whenever I ask her anything, unless it involves money and then she glares and launches into a rant. I know that money is tight at the moment but it doesn't mean that I don't have needs. And, according to Mum's GLITZ magazine, what I need right now is some Starshine fake tan to put the spring into my spring. Sadly, Mum didn't agree when I showed her the article at breakfast.

"I've told you before not to read my magazines, Cassidy," she said, before I'd even got to number three of TEN TAN-TASTIC REASONS TO FAKE IT. "You're too young to be worrying about fake tan, anyway. You'll just have to put up with being pale."

Huh. It's alright for her, she hardly ever leaves the house and when she does, people are so busy cooing over the twins that they barely even notice she's there. Actually, that's probably a good thing since next to her, even vampires look tanned. I, on the other hand, have less than five weeks until the St Jude's Secondary School May Ball and I refuse to go to it looking like Draco Malfoy's paler sister.

"But—"

"Forget it, Cassie," she snapped, laying a snoozing Ethel down in the Moses basket and picking up her long-cold cup of tea. "Don't think I've forgotten the HIGHLIGHTS FROM HELL incident."

And that was typical too. I mean, we all make mistakes, right? Some people might encounter more than their fair share of little hiccups (like – I don't know – leaving a home highlighter kit on for a teensy bit too long and turning their hair a bright, brassy orange, maybe) but that doesn't mean they need to be reminded of them

ALL THE TIME. Especially when one little trip to the hairdresser sorted everything out and didn't cost THAT much. But my mum doesn't believe in letting bygones be bygones. Oh no, she never forgets ANYTHING.

Summoning my inner goddess of calm, I dropped my crusts under the table for Rolo (AKA Destructo-Puppy), and got up. "I have to go."

Dad raised an eyebrow as he swayed. "Don't you want a lift?"

I shook my head. "I'm meeting Molly and Shenice. See you later."

I almost left the kitchen without giving the babies a goodbye kiss, but I caught a glimpse of Joshua's slumbering face snuffling over Dad's shoulder and, just like that, my annoyance evaporated. I dashed back and dropped a gentle kiss on each of their foreheads. While I was still feeling affectionate, I dipped my head to peck Mum's cheek too.

"Have a good day," I whispered.

She smiled, and her eyes lit up in a tired sort of way that made me feel a bit guilty. At least we get to escape the madhouse each day; she is trapped here in a never-ending nightmare of nuclear nappies and a mountain of baby wipes, with only CBeebies for company. For the gazillionth time since the twins arrived, I resolved to be more helpful. Or at the very least, less fake-tan obsessed.

"Thanks, Cass," Mum said, as Ethel scrunched up her nose and started to cry. "You too."

I'm not ashamed to admit that I ducked out then. I love Joshua and Ethel to bits, I really do, but they're SO high maintenance. What I need is a door to another world in the back of my wardrobe, a place where the animals talk and don't mistake your shoes for pudding.

The cool thing about having BFFs you've known since you were four years old is that you can rely on them to make you feel better. Like when Molly used her dad's nose hair trimmer to give her teddy bear a Mohican and we shaved the fur off ours to stop her crying. Or when Shenice's half-brother downloaded a virus onto their mum's laptop and blamed it on her – we were totally there for her and even offered to write to the European Court of Human Rights to complain about the injustice. So I was pretty confident that Molly and Shenice were going to be one hundred per cent sympathetic when I mentioned my state of extreme exhaustion on the way to school.

"Babies cry, Cassie," Molly sighed, rolling her eyes as though she'd heard it all before. "I'm surprised you're not used to it by now."

I screwed my face up in a sarky smile. For a so-called BFF, she wasn't being very understanding. Then I remembered she was an only child and had never suffered the delights of an infant alarm clock. "I notice you haven't been for a sleepover since the twins arrived," I replied. "Maybe you should try it and see how you get on with a sleep debt the size of Everest!"

We carried on squabbling all the way to the school gates. At least, me and Molly did. Shenice didn't say much, she just sort of trailed along next to us as we argued. And after a little while, it sank into my frazzled brain that something was wrong.

I nudged Molly. "What's up, Shen? Don't tell me you're sleep deprived as well?"

She shrugged. "No."

"So what's going on?" Molly asked.

Shenice looked around the playground, as though checking no one was close enough to overhear. "Pinky promise you'll keep this between us, right?" she whispered. We nodded and she went on. "You know when you think you know someone but it turns out you don't really know them at all?"

"You mean like that time when we thought we saw Ziggy from The Droids and begged him to sign our faces but it turned out not to be him and then we couldn't get the ink off?" Molly said, frowning.

Shenice scowled. "No, not like that. I – look, just forget it."

I stopped walking. There's this unwritten friendship law between the three of us which means we share EVERYTHING. It had to be something serious if Shenice didn't want to talk about it. "No, we won't forget it," I said. "Something is obviously wrong and we want to help."

She didn't speak for a minute. Then, to my horror, her big brown eyes filled with tears. "It's nothing really. Just that my mum has gone out every Thursday evening for the last five weeks."

Molly looked blank and even I was having trouble working out why Shenice was so upset – her older brother was usually around when her mum wasn't so she didn't have to fend for herself.

"So what?" Molly said. "Maybe she's a Bingo Babe. My aunt got really into it when they went on holiday to Brighton last year and my uncle had to ban her from going to the arcade on the pier."

Shenice shook her head. "It's worse than that. I – I think she might have started dating again."

My mouth fell open in an O of understanding. Shenice's parents had split up years ago and her dad had moved in with a woman called Gloria almost immediately. Shenice didn't really like her but as she only saw her dad once a month, it wasn't much of an issue. Her mum, on the other hand, had been single ever since. The thought of her going on dates and possibly meeting someone who might become part of Shenice's future was officially scary biscuits.

Molly looked unconvinced. "Are you sure she isn't playing bingo? Auntie Eleni told Uncle Dimitri that she was going jogging but really she was at the pier the whole time. My dad said it was the only way she'd ever lose twenty pounds, and Auntie Eleni didn't speak to him for a week."

"I might have checked Mum's phone," Shenice admitted, going a bit red. "She's been texting this Julio about meeting up and I'm sure that's where she's been sneaking off to."

Eep. We had a waiter called Julio on our family holiday to Tenerife last year but it wasn't the kind of name I'd heard a lot in Windsor, apart from when I got caught up in a Spanish tour group outside the castle and nearly ended up on their coach back to Barcelona.

"There could be an innocent explanation," I said, trying to make her feel better. "I'm sure it's all a big misunderstanding."

"I found this letter she'd written in her notebook," Shenice went on. "In a language that definitely wasn't English and looked a lot like Spanish."

That sounded bad. As far as I knew, Shen's mum didn't even speak Spanish.

"She must really like him if she's learning a whole new language," Molly said quietly.

"But that's just it," Shenice cried. "What if Julio and Mum like each other so much that they get married and I have to move to Spain or something?"

I didn't know what to say and from the look on Molly's face, neither did she. It was a horrible prospect. "At least you like paella," I managed.

The bell rang, and for the first time ever, we walked to our class in silence. Poor Shenice – Spain is nice to visit but I'm not sure I'd want to live there. And my parents can be awful and embarrassing and totally uncool but at least neither of them is secretly dating someone called Julio.

I read this book once where the heroine escaped from her miserable home life by running away to join the circus, although she was this amazing gymnast so maybe that had something to do with it. Shenice's thing is swimming but I don't think there's much call for that as a performance art. She could probably get a job as a clown — one of those really sad-looking ones — I bet you don't need any qualifications to do it and even a life of custard-pie dodging would be better than a stepdad she doesn't want.

I am starting to feel very bad for Shenice. My family might lurch from one sleep-deprived crisis to another but we just about keep it together. I hope that's the way it stays.

✱ Don't pay salon prices for luxurious hair treatments – use everyday foods like EGGS, VINEGAR or BEER as a conditioner! We promise you'll never have felt anything like it.

(Vinegar? Will smell like chip shop, surely? Yuck!)

✱ Forget EXPENSIVE spot creams – baby's NAPPY RASH CREAM works a treat!

(Excellent, one thing there's no shortage of in this house.)

✱ Nail varnish gone GLOOPY? Pop it in the FRIDGE and it'll be as good as new.

✱ Rinse and dry an old mascara wand and use it to apply VASELINE to your lashes overnight. You'll soon have THICK LOVELY LASHES without the need for costly falsies!

(Next time, do not poke eye with slimy finger.)

* Save £££ by CUTTING your own fringe.

* BROKEN a fake nail? Salons would love to fix it for a small fee but you can make your own thrifty repairs using SUPERGLUE. Just a tiny dab does it!

* Slather VASELINE over your feet before you go to sleep and kiss goodbye to ugly hard skin.

(No no no no no no no no no no no. NO. Remember last DIY hair SOS.)

(Last time Dad Superglued something, he stuck his fingers to the washing machine door. Just saying.)

(Put socks on feet next time to avoid DANCING ON ICE routine when going for a midnight wee.)

CHAPTER THREE

I'm not sure GLITZ was right when they said a "GORGEOUS GOLDEN GLOW" was "ONLY A FINGERTIP AWAY". It's certainly all OVER my fingertips, and underneath my nails, although I'd call it more of a yucky brown. Maybe if I'd been able to get the actual proper Starshine stuff, things might have gone better, but they didn't sell it in the little chemist next to the doctor's surgery. It always smells of lavender and old people in there. I am guessing there isn't much call for fake tan among the OAPs of Windsor because we looked for ages before Shenice finally found a few dusty bottles of Go Glow! in between the pads for ladies who pee when they laugh and the elasticated support stockings. The bottle is undeniably orange, which is hopefully not the colour I will turn or Mum will definitely notice. The instructions had rubbed off but as far as I can tell, you just put it on and – HEY PRESTO! – a few hours later, you are a vision of sultry-skinned healthiness. I am trying it out on my legs first and then it will be all systems go for Operation Tantastic in time for the May Ball next month.

Mum didn't even bat an eyelid when I said I was going to bed early with a headache – yet more evidence that either she doesn't listen to me or she no longer cares. It doesn't matter; by morning, I will have beautiful bronzed legs and my days of looking like I am a member of the undead will be over.

Omg.

OMG.

O. M. ACTUAL. G — my legs are stripy! Seriously,
they look like manky sticks of rock, without the minty
sweetness. I must have stuck to the duvet cover while
I slept, because that is all stripy too. And I smell like the
inside of a biscuit barrel — GLITZ didn't mention THAT in
their article. Don't ask what's going on with my knees — for
some reason they are much darker than my shins and look
like a pair of squeezed-out teabags. How can I go to school
like this? People will think I'm Tigger's long-lost sister.

Okay, deep breaths. Maybe a shower will help.
It cannot make things any worse.

The shower has not helped. The streaks are still
there and my legs are now red underneath the stripes
from where I used a whole bottle of Mum's Sanctuary
Body Scrub. I do smell slightly less like a custard

34

cream but that is no consolation
when I look like a sunburned
giraffe. There is definitely no
way I can wear the skirt and
ankle sock combo I had planned
for today, which means I will have to

steal some of Mum's saggy opaque tights and hope they
hide my shame. Of course, if girls were allowed to wear
trousers at ST CRUDE'S, I'd be fine, but we are ruled by
a dictatorship that denies us basic rights like these. It's
about time someone made a stand; we should throw down
our glitter pens and demand equality. It'll be like LES
MISÉRABLES, but with less singing. And after the
revolution, all comrades will be free to wear trousers.

I am SO glad today is over. Liam caught me stuffing my
sheets into the washing machine this morning and tried
to drop me in it by wrinkling his nose up and asking
loudly if I'd slept in the McVitie's factory. Then he

threatened to take a photo of my legs and send it in to JOJ, whatever that is – some stupid band website, probably. Honestly, he is such a moron – if he does anything to embarrass me I will saw through the strings on his precious guitar using my Hello Kitty nail file. Rolo was almost as bad – he kept barking and trying to lick my legs through the tights. I'm amazed Mum didn't clock on. I suppose there are some benefits to having a sleep-deprived mother, after all. Pre-twins Mum would have busted me in a heartbeat.

I confessed what had happened to Molly and Shenice on the way to school – naturally, they thought it was HILARIOUS. It's alright for them. Molly's parents are Greek and Shenice is mixed race so neither know the pain of milk-bottle legs. Mind you, the horror of tiger stripes is infinitely worse.

Our Citizenship lesson was actually quite useful for once today – I asked Miss Hemsworth what the best way to overthrow an oppressive regime was and she said it depends on the country. In some places the military launch a coup, but I don't think the British Army would be much help in the battle for equal trousers. Then she said we have this government website where you can start a petition and if it gets a certain number of signatures, your petition has to be read out in the House of Commons. Then the politicians might have a debate about it. So I went into the library at lunchtime and looked it up online and it is all true, although you need one hundred thousand signatures before MPs will discuss it. But I reckon I have to start somewhere so I lodged an e-petition with Her Majesty's Government to say that girls should be allowed to wear trousers at St Jude's. I sent the link to Shenice and Molly and even my Auntie Jane, and they've all said they'll send it on to everyone they know.

With a bit of luck, the time for equal trousers could be just around the corner!

E-PETITION

Allow Girls To Wear Trousers
At St Jude's Secondary

Imagine it is a freezing cold morning. All around you, boys are cosy in their thick trousers, but your legs only have tights between them and the cold, because you are a girl. At St Jude's Secondary School, this happens every day. It is like living in the Dark Ages and it's not fair!

All students should have the right to clothing equality! I would like the government to force the Governors of St Jude's (AKA Evil Clothing Police) to change their medieval rules and grant girls the right to trouser up if they want to. Sign my petition to get justice for girls!

Created by: Cassidy Bond

SIGN THIS PETITION

First name:

Last name:

Email:

Number of signatures: 126

CHAPTER FOUR

The weirdest thing happened today. We were sitting on the steps outside the science block at lunchtime when Kelly Anderson from Year Ten came up to us. Well, I say Kelly but actually it was her and two of her fellow goddesses, descending from the heights of Mount Popular to slum it with us mere mortals. Kelly is totally gorgeous — Liam has a crush the size of Australia on her and so do most of the other boys in school. The really annoying thing is, not only is she Disney Princess pretty, she's really nice and everyone likes her. She's smart too —

she runs **HEY JUDE'S!**, the school magazine. So when she stopped in front of us, I knew without the slightest little doubt that I was going to show myself up. Or, if by some miracle I managed to keep my cool, either Molly or Shenice were sure to lose theirs. When Rolo gets really nervous or excited, a little bit of wee comes out — imagine if one of us did **THAT**...

"You're Cassidy Bond, yeah?" Kelly said.

OMG, she knew my name! An image of Rolo popped into my head, a telltale puddle by his paws. Crossing one foot over the other, I nodded carefully.

"The one who started that petition about girls wearing trousers at school?" she went on, her eyes narrowing.

My blood ran cold — how did she know about that? I mean, an amazing one hundred and twenty-six people have signed my petition already, but I didn't think Kelly was one of them. What had I done, offended her fashion sense or something? Beside me, Molly and Shenice were exchanging looks and fidgeting.

Then the unthinkable happened – Kelly smiled. "That was a pretty cool thing to do."

All the breath went out of me in a **WHOOSH** and Shenice did this squeak thing.

"Er, thanks," I managed, nudging Shen before she embarrassed us. "I just thought we should have the choice."

Kelly was nodding and her wing girls were copying her. "Exactly. Listen, I need a Year Seven correspondent for the school paper, someone who'll do what needs to be done in the search for a good story." She paused and looked me straight in the eye. "Are you in?"

Was I in? Is a
unicorn horn POINTY?

"Could be," I said,
trying to sound like it
was the kind of offer I got
all the time. "Yeah, why not?"

"Great," she said, smiling again. "We meet at
lunchtime on Mondays, in the English block. See you
there."

She walked off, leaving me staring after her in
a daze. Had Kelly Anderson just called me cool or was
I dreaming?

"Not unless we're all having the same dream," Molly
said, and I realized I must have spoken out loud. "Wow.
You're going to be a member of The Press. You'll have
access all areas."

42

Okay, so access all areas of St Crude's didn't mean much but it was still the most exciting thing to happen to me this term. I grinned, unable to believe my luck. Actually, I still can't. Wait until Liam finds out! Ever since his band, **WOLF BRETHREN**, was asked to play at the May Ball, he's been swaggering round like he's some kind of Rock God. Knowing he's not the Bond everyone at St Crude's is talking about any more might just take the bounce out of his bungee.

The scream monsters woke me up AGAIN at ridiculous o'clock. Luckily, I was having this horrific nightmare where Mum grew a moustache and became a bingo caller, so I didn't mind for once. I don't remember going back to sleep but I must have done because when I looked at the clock again, it was half past eight, which is practically midday in the twins' book. For one toe-curling second, I thought I was late for school, and then I remembered it was Saturday. And THEN I remembered that I am no longer boring old Cassidy Bond, I am C Bond – STAR REPORTER, and decided I'd better find out what a journalist does.

I walked to the paper shop, planning on picking up THE TIMES, THE GUARDIAN and the MIRROR, but the new copy of GLITZ had TWENTY WAYS TO LOVE YOUR LIFE on the cover so I bought that instead, pretending to the newsagent it was for Mum. It's practically research – who is to say that Kelly hasn't recruited me to be St Jude's celebrity gossip correspondent, anyway?

Dad was downstairs with the twins when I got back, trying to give them both a bottle at the same time and failing badly. I took pity on him and grabbed Ethel, after I'd conducted a secret sniff test, of course. Dad's rule is that whoever is holding a twin when they make a stinky is the one who changes the nappy and I've been caught out that way before.

"Thanks," he said, wiping the milk off the end of his nose. "I thought I'd let your mum have a bit of a lie-in."

Every now and then, I wonder what my mum sees in my dad, especially when he is crooning Elvis songs in his awful white suit and stupid black wig, but he's alright sometimes. When he's not dressed up as the King, OBVIOUSLY.

"That's nice," I said. "According to this study I read about in GLITZ, women who get six or more hours of sleep a night are happier, healthier and live longer."

"Good to know," Dad said, giving me the thumbs up. "If she's in a good mood later, I might talk to her about having a summer holiday this year."

My ears pricked up. Liam and I had talked about the chances of going ANYWHERE good when school broke up and we'd decided we had more chance of winning the lottery. "Really?"

Dad nodded. "I think we can manage a couple of weeks somewhere sunny."

That sounded promising. Two weeks in the sun would definitely take the edge off my painfully white skin, although I hoped it wasn't Spain – that would really rub Shenice's nose in it, especially since Shenice was positive her mum had been on another date with the mysterious Julio. I opened my mouth to suggest Florida but Dad beat me to it.

"So how does a de luxe camper van in Cornwall sound? We can even take Rolo."

I stared at him in shock, all thoughts of Mickey Mouse flying out of my head. "A camper van? All of us? In Cornwall?"

"Okay, a caravan then. We can't go too far — imagine flying anywhere with these two."

I pictured a long flight with the Wide Awake Club and shuddered. Okay, so maybe Florida was out, but a caravan **ANYWHERE** with them would mean even less sleep than we got now. It was the stuff of holiday nightmares.

"Come on, it'll be fun," Dad said, picking Joshua up and patting his back until he let out the kind of burp that sets off avalanches. "With a bit of luck there'll be entertainment on the campsite. And if there isn't, I can volunteer my services and earn a few quid at the same time."

I stared gloomily at Ethel, guzzling her milk in
blissful ignorance of the embarrassment in her future.
Liam wouldn't be impressed when I broke the news,
either. It is going to be the Worst Holiday Ever. Normally
I can rely on Mum to stop Dad from embarrassing us,
but she is living on borrowed brains. I am telling you,
if Dad is serious about getting up onstage while we
are there, I am definitely not going.

I wonder when Zippo's Circus
is next in town? Maybe Shenice and
I can do a double act.

I woke up this morning to discover my e-petition has
gone totally crazy. It has over three hundred signatures
from complete strangers, in places like Glasgow and
Belfast and Scunthorpe. There was even one from this
girl in Pratt's Bottom, saying that I have inspired her to
start her own school campaign, although I'm not sure

there is really a place called Pratt's Bottom and wonder
if it is actually Dad, trying to be supportive. Yesterday,
he called me the Che Guevara of St Jude's. I thought that
was some bloke from off the telly until I tapped his name
into a search engine and found out that he was this
amazing revolutionary who really rocked the beret and
got a lot of stuff done. Liam was all grumpy about it,
saying it was a waste of time and that the school will never
listen to me, but secretly I think he is impressed. I am
starting to think that we might actually get enough
signatures to make the Prime Minister notice – imagine
that! St Jude's would have to change the rules then.

Molly and Shenice came over after lunch and we
planned what we would wear to march on Downing Street –
trousers, obviously, but I had this idea about getting my
mum to make one gigantic pair that we could all wear at
the same time. Molly said we could probably go for the
world record of most people in one pair of trousers, which
sounds a bit warm. I go all red-faced when I'm hot and

I wouldn't want to be on the front page of all the newspapers looking like a tomato. It reminded me of Liam's threat to send my stripy legs in to that website, so I looked it up and it turns out he wasn't kidding — JOJ actually exists!

It stands for JUICE ON JUDE'S and seems to be some kind of blog about our school. There are all these funny stories and pictures about everyone. Some of them are pretty funny, like the photos of the Year Seven raft-building exercise in Wales that sank as soon as it was launched. I don't know whose idea JUICE ON JUDE'S was but it MUST be someone at school. Who though? No one knows. We spent over an hour reading the old posts and giggling at the pictures. There was no sign of my stripy legs on there, thank goodness — maybe Liam is only mostly moron.

Now that my fake tan disaster has faded and I am no longer part Oompa Loompa, I am really looking forward to my first school mag meeting tomorrow. Who knows, this could be the start of a twin career as a wrong-righting journalist and a political activist. Maybe Fighting Social Injustice is going to be my Thing!

Note to Self:

* Buy beret.

* Ask Liam who writes JOJ.

To: <u>BondGirl007</u>

From: <u>Pam.Postlethwaite@BabyBaby</u>

Dear Cassie,

Thanks for your email – great to hear from you! Congratulations on becoming a big sister to your baby brother and sister! We love twins here at BabyBaby and it sounds like you do too.

To answer your question, it's perfectly normal for babies to chew things when they start teething. Unfortunately, this can include fingers, as you rather painfully discovered. I'm afraid I don't have any suggestions to prevent your dog from running off with the babies' rattles – he sounds like rather a handful! I am very sorry to hear that he ate the bell from your sister's teddy bear – I'm not a vet but I doubt the tinkling sound you hear when you walk him is anything to do with the missing bell.

Lastly, many babies start to sleep for longer when they move onto solid food around six months of age, so there is light at the end of the sleep-deprivation tunnel!

Good luck and enjoy being a big sister!

All best wishes,

Pam Postlethwaite
BabyBaby – the website with all the answers

CHAPTER FIVE

I think I may have died and gone to heaven. Not only did Kelly Anderson nod hello to me in the corridor this morning, but Nathan Crossfield stopped by my table in registration today to congratulate me on becoming the Year Seven school mag correspondent. The actual Nathan Crossfield, a boy of such sub-zero coolness that even the sixth-formers know who he is, and the only boy in the world (apart from Liam) who knows I used to be into fairies in a **BIG** way. The gut-wrenching memory of Rolo dropping a pair of fairy knickers at Nathan's feet last year might stop me from sleeping at night, if the twins didn't already have that covered.

Anyway, I try to keep it quiet but I've had the mightiest crush on Nathan for most of the year, ever since I became an ACCIDENTAL GENIUS and our team won the regional heat of Kids' Quiz last autumn. For a few days, me, Nathan, Rebecca and Bilal were famous and even reached page six of the WINDSOR RECORDER. I spent a lot of time studying with them (well, they studied and I daydreamed about Nathan) and we were all totally gutted when we lost in the national final. Team St Jude's split up after that and, without an excuse to hang out together, Nathan and I didn't talk as much — it's pretty hard to stay mates when one of you is the star striker on the under-fourteens school football squad, School Council rep and all-round Mr Popular, while the other smells permanently of baby sick. So I went back to mostly staring at him across the classroom and daydreaming. Which is why I couldn't stop grinning when he walked over to where I was sitting with Molly and Shenice, and also why I pretended it was no big deal.

"OMG, he fancies you!" Shenice squealed as we headed to maths. "He totally does."

"Shut up!" I hissed, looking around to check no one had heard. "He was just being nice."

"Did you see that thing on JUICE ON JUDE'S about him and Susie Carr in Year Eight?" Molly said, her eyes widening. "It said they went to see ZOMBIE PROM II together."

Shenice frowned. "I thought that was a fifteen."

I'd read the same story about Susie on JOJ last night and it had ruined my evening. In fact, the thought of Nathan going to the cinema with ANYONE made me feel a bit queasy. "It is. Liam tried to go last week and the cashier told him library cards don't count as ID."

"Susie does look older," Molly pointed out. "I bet she got the tickets and he got the popcorn." →

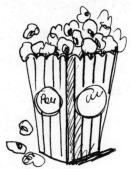

I wasn't sure JOJ was right – Nathan might be the nearest thing Year Seven has to a superstar but he's still a year younger than Susie Carr. She's really pretty too; there must be loads of boys dying to take her to see zombies in frocks. At least I hoped there were.

"It doesn't matter anyway," I insisted in a low voice, as we filed into the classroom for a whole hour of Mr Peterson droning on about number sequences and equations. "He doesn't fancy me and I don't fancy him. We're just two people who used to be on a quiz team together."

Shenice and Molly exchanged a look.

"Uh-huh," Shenice said, grinning. "Like Molly doesn't fancy Liam."

Now it was Molly's turn to go pink. I don't know why she was embarrassed – it's no secret that she thinks my moronic brother is cute. She practically lived at my house last autumn, when the ST JUDE'S HAS GOT TALENT! competition was hotting up, and she is definitely WOLF BRETHREN's number-one fan.

"Liam and I respect each other as artists," she said haughtily. "We'd never let our relationship get in the way of the music."

I rolled my eyes – she'd clearly been watching the rock biopics on Sky Arts again. It's the kind of thing Liam and my dad say all the time when they're talking about crusty old bands like The Beatles. The thing is, Liam and

Molly don't have much of a relationship, unless you count him asking her to do crappy stuff like hand out flyers when they've got a gig coming up. But it doesn't matter how many times I tell her he's just using her, she still thinks he's amazing.

"Whatever," I muttered, sitting down and preparing for the festival of boredom to begin. My attention drifted almost immediately and came to rest on Nathan, seated a few tables away. What I'd told Molly and Shenice was partly true – when we'd hung out, it HAD only ever been as friends. But that was only because Nathan saw me as another mate, someone he could have a laugh with, a solid team player even though we weren't actually team-mates any more. Now that I am a reporter, he might just see that there is more to me than a mental dog and an all-encompassing knowledge of Hogwarts. He might notice that I am a girl.

I couldn't swallow my tuna salad baguette fast enough at lunchtime. With one eye on the clock, I wolfed it down and left Molly and Shenice still eating while I hurried over to the English block and my first official meeting as a journalist. I'd brought a new pen and dug out a half-used notepad and everything. ➜

I don't mind admitting that I felt as though my lunch was going to come back and choke me when I saw them all sitting around the classroom. Some of the coolest kids in school were there, the kind of people who wouldn't normally know I existed. But there was also Jimmy Nelson from Year Eight, who is the geekiest geek ever. No one seemed to be making a joke about him being there so I guessed he was part of the group.

Kelly came over the second she saw me hovering in the doorway.

"Cass, come in!" she said, a welcoming grin on her face. "You don't mind if I call you Cass, do you?"

I didn't mind. I was so in awe she could have called me Bruce Bogtrotter and I wouldn't have minded, to be honest.

"Hi," I squeaked. "I'm not late, am I?"

"No, we don't start until Mr Bearman gets here," she explained. "He supervises, although what we decide to cover is completely down to us. Let me introduce you to the press gang."

The press gang – how cool did that sound? Like THE AVENGERS, but with pens instead of weapons, and school uniforms. Kelly knows all the journalisty slang – I might start using a few phrases myself.

The rest of my fellow press gangers were seated

around the tables or on them. Kelly worked her way around the room and, one by one, they all waved and said hi. There was Alex Jones from Year Eight, Nisha Choudhury and Kieran Sanderson from Year Nine, Mel Wallis from Year Ten and a boy called Toby from Year Eleven who I'd never seen before in my life. And Jimmy, of course, but he was sniggering over a Macbook Pro and didn't even look up.

"Alex and Nisha cover school sports, Mel does all the arty stuff and Kieran is our music expert," Kelly said. "We all keep an eye out for stories specific to our year groups too – the human interest stuff."

"Like when Team St Jude's won the regional Kids' Quiz," Mel said, smiling, and I decided I liked her.

"And when you blew it in the final," Alex added, and I decided I didn't like him. We'd finished in fifth place, out of the WHOLE COUNTRY, which was pretty amazing as far as I was concerned. But this was my first-ever magazine meeting and I wanted them to like me, so I smiled and ignored him.

Mr Bearman appeared in the doorway. I saw Kelly's eyes flash at Jimmy and he slammed the lid of the laptop so fast I swear his fingers blurred. What was that all about?

"Good afternoon, everyone," Mr Bearman said, closing the door behind himself and perching on the edge of a table. His gaze came to rest on me. "And welcome to our newest recruit. Great to see you here, Cassie."

Mr Bearman teaches me for English and is totally my favourite teacher. It was thanks to him that I joined Team St Jude's in the first place (although if I'm totally honest, it was Nathan who did the persuading). Mr Bearman's always been really encouraging. He's pretty much the best teacher in the ENTIRE WORLD so having him in charge of the school magazine is completely brilliant.

"Hello, sir."

"So, what have we got for this month's edition, Kelly?"

Kelly nodded to Jimmy and he scurried to the front of the classroom, a data stick in his hand. So that explained his presence among the cool kids, I decided – he was the technical support. Within seconds, he'd opened up a presentation on the interactive whiteboard and had backed away, giving Kelly centre stage.

"Sport," she said, clicking on the first slide. "This week, we've got the inter-school netball tournament, the house football cup and next week it's the swimming gala. Nish and Al have got the skinny on those."

The skinny? I supposed she meant that sporty people were usually thin but it seemed like an odd way to describe them. She clicked the mouse again and a picture of Liam and his band mates popped up. I cringed. "WOLF BRETHREN are St Jude's hard-rock answer to The Droids. Since they're also the resident band for the lower school's May Ball, Kieran has got the scoop on their likes, dislikes and musical inspiration."

Huh, the thing Liam likes best is stuffing his face with pepperoni pizza, but he doesn't use a scoop. I kept my mouth shut, though, in case I showed myself up. Liam had already warned me not to talk about him and the band. Besides, I didn't want him to think I admitted he was my brother.

Kelly glanced over at me. "Then we've got Cassidy's efforts to change the St Jude's rules about school uniform." A slide appeared with a screenshot of the petition on it and I saw with a jolt that it had over five hundred signatures on it. My little petition, up there with my name on it, and all those people had signed to say they agreed with me. Who'd have thought it would grow so fast?

"Ah yes," Mr Bearman said, smiling at me. "Quite the revolutionary, Cassidy."

The others were staring at me and I was glad I'd decided to leave my beret at home. "Suppose so, sir."

"Plus we've got the regular stuff – the horoscopes, crossword and adverts. Mrs Armstrong has got the lowdown on dealing with exam stress too. Anyone want to pitch anything else?"

Huh, Mrs Armstrong is in her fifties – if she got low down, she wouldn't get back up again. I listened as the gang tossed ideas around. Mel wanted to write a piece about the art exhibition Year Ten were doing for Parents'

Evening. I sat in silence, wondering whether my fellow Year Sevens were doing anything cool. I'd have to dig around – hey, maybe that was what the scoop was for.

"Sounds like another excellent issue," Mr Bearman said, after a few more minutes' discussion. "The deadline for copy is two weeks from today and the magazine will go out the week after the May Ball. Good work, everyone."

I blinked. Copy? What did we have to copy? Teachers usually go NUTSO if you do that – I remember what happened when Shenice and I forgot to do our History homework. We copied Molly's and she'd written about how the Battle of Hating was won by William the Conker, so we did too. Our teacher gave us this big long lecture about how we were only cheating ourselves and how slackers never amounted to anything. Surely Mr Bearman didn't actually mean we should copy stuff to publish in HEY JUDE'S! Because I wasn't making that mistake again.

Mr Bearman must have seen my confusion because he came over. "Everything okay, Cassie?"

I didn't want to look like an idiot so I put on an expression of breezy confidence. "Oh yes, sir. I'm just off to copy something now. Where do you keep the scoop?"

He stared at me for a long moment. "Ah. I thought Kelly might have explained a few basic journalist terms to you but apparently not. A scoop means a story we get before everyone else. Copy is what we call the writing that goes into the magazine. It doesn't mean we copy someone else's work – that's called plagiarism and it's against the law."

I nodded as though it all made sense, but really I was wondering why he couldn't have just said "the deadline for articles is two weeks from today". I can see there is a lot more to this journalism business than I thought, but I am determined to make it my Thing. Imagine having my name splashed across the front page in a searing article on the source of the terrible smell in the PE changing rooms – I'd be totally famous at St Jude's and maybe it would even get picked up by the WINDSOR RECORDER. Or maybe I could uncover the person behind JUICE ON JUDE'S – I'd probably win an award for investigative skills. Then perhaps Liam would have to stop acting like he is the only one in our family with any talent.

My time to shine is on its way, I can feel it!

To: <u>BondGirl007</u>

From: <u>Happy Sands Enquiries</u>

Hi Cassie,

Thanks for getting in touch – I'm delighted to hear that you and your family will be joining us at Happy Sands Newquay this summer!

In answer to your question, we have a packed season of superstars lined up to entertain you all week long. Unfortunately, that doesn't quite stretch to include The Droids but I know you'll be excited to hear that we do have Jeffy Jeff, from brand-new local boy band Twice As Nice, and a side-splitting ventriloquism act starring Kimmy the Koala, fresh from the smash-hit TV show, Jungle Jingles. And don't forget, there'll be Kidz Karaoke run by Nelly the Elephant and Treasure

Hunts with Captain Pigeon every day. With fun like that in store, I bet you can't wait to come and see us!! I'll be sure to keep an eye out for you in July!

Sunshine and smiles,

Tracy Cooper
Head of Children's Entertainment, Happy Sands Holiday Villages PLC

SOMEONE. KILL. ME. NOW.

CHAPTER SIX

Wow. What a week! Not only did my petition gain even more signatures (squee!) but Nathan said hi to me every morning. In fact, this week has been so good that I didn't even make a fuss when Rolo ate my new beret, especially since Liam says it looks like I am balancing a cow pat on my head when I wear it.

It's also totally amazing being in the press gang! Mum says I should learn something called shorthand to speed up my note taking, which seems to be like Egyptian hieroglyphics and only proves how old my mother is. Kelly asked me to shadow Nisha's coverage of the netball tournament after school on Wednesday, so I got to hang out with her and all her cool Year Nine mates and absolutely none of them drew any weird squiggly pictures instead of writing. They asked me about my dress for the May Ball and I tried to be all vague but the truth is, I haven't dared ask Mum for one yet, even though it is only two weeks to the ball. She'll probably suggest I make it out of the twins' old sleepsuits.

By Friday, I was so exhausted that I looked like a raccoon. When Shenice invited me and Molly to sleep over at her house, I couldn't get over there fast enough. So what if I had to sleep on a blow-up bed, or that Molly's crazy ringlets might try to smother me in the night, like they always do? The odds of someone waking me up by screaming for milk at two in the morning were a lot lower than at my own house. At least I hoped they were.

With one thing and another, I haven't seen as much of Molly and Shenice as I usually do. Tucked up in Shen's room in our pyjamas with The Droids blasting out, I could tell they were really keen to hear all about my new career as a journalist – every time I mentioned Kelly or Nisha or said the word "journo", they'd sort of smile at each other, as though my success was their success. I've been worried that I might be making them feel a bit jealous. Their lives aren't exactly overflowing with excitement, after all – Shenice's mum is still hanging out with Julio every Thursday evening and Molly still spends every spare moment obsessing over my brother. I don't want them to think I'm rubbing their noses in my new-found popularity, but maybe it will help take their minds off their problems.

"Listen, I've got something to ask you," Molly interrupted when I started to tell them about Kelly's fruit system for rating how juicy a story was. "It's really important."

"Yeah?" I said. "Although I have to tell you that if it's about an ongoing story in HEY JUDE'S! my lips are sealed."

Molly scowled. "Will you shut up about that for a minute? It's about Liam, anyway."

I sat back, a bit surprised at the irritation in her voice. Maybe I HAD been going on about my new career too much after all. "What about him? He's still a moron, in case you were wondering."

She ignored me. "I read on JUICE ON JUDE'S that Max is moving to Leeds next week. Tell me it's not true!"

I guessed she meant the bass guitar
player from WOLF BRETHREN — he's called
Max — but honestly, what was she asking
me for? I'm the last person to know
anything about Liam these days — he's
always rehearsing. JOJ is my new
guilty pleasure — I know I
shouldn't love it but it's the
first thing I check when I get
home each day — but I must
have missed the bit about Max
in amongst all the other gossip. Or maybe I have
trained my brain to ignore all WOLF BRETHREN
references. Whatever the reason, I was drawing a blank
until a memory stirred at the back of my mind — hadn't
Liam said something to Dad about auditions for a new
band member next week? Maybe that had something
to do with it. "Er...it might be. Why?"

"WHY?" she exploded, so loudly that Shenice and

I jumped. "It's only the first nail in **WOLF BRETHREN**'s coffin, that's all! It's like when Josie left The Go-Go Bunnies – the beginning of the end. I can't believe you didn't tell me!"

And to my utter astonishment, she burst into tears. Shenice and I stared at each other, unsure what to say. I mean, I know Molly loves the band but this was off the scale, even for her.

"Liam doesn't seem very worried," I said uncertainly, pulling a confused face at Shenice over Molly's bowed head. I racked my brains for details of the conversation he'd had with my dad. "He said bass players are two a penny and he hoped some really hot girls would apply."

Shenice was making a desperate, one-handed cutting motion across her throat but it was too late. Molly stopped crying mid-sob and raised her head to look at me through narrowed eyes.

"What?"

Ooops.

"But mostly, they want someone good," I babbled, going for damage limitation. "And the main thing is that they get the best person for the job, right?"

The silence was broken by a knock at the door. Shenice's mum poked her head into the room. She was wearing a sombrero. "CHOCOLATE CALIENTE PARA MIS CHICAS!"

Shenice groaned and covered her face with her hands. "Mum, you're from Basingstoke, not Barcelona. Speak English!"

"There's nothing wrong with bringing a bit of

sunshine into our lives," Shen's mum said, holding out the tray. She's really lovely but she does treat us like we're little kids. The tray had three mugs of hot chocolate on it, piled high with cream and marshmallows. Next to them was a bowl of pastel-coloured Iced Gems and a big bag of Haribo. Not that I'm complaining, of course – you're never too old for gummy bears and tiny biscuits.

"I thought you might be peckish," she said. Then she saw Molly's tear-stained face and frowned. "Is everything okay?"

"Everything's fine, Mum," Shenice said, letting out a heavy sigh. "Just go."

"Are you sure?" Mrs Coleman said, looking at Molly sympathetically. "Is it boy trouble?"

"Mum!" Shenice shouted and I thought she might

actually throw the tray across the room. "Molly is fine, we are fine, please leave us alone."

"Alright," she said and turned to go. "Make sure you bring those mugs down when you're finished, Shenice. The last cup you left up here started a new civilization under your bed." The door clicked in its frame but not before we heard her call, "ADIOS, AMIGOS!"

Shenice made a weird growly noise as she handed out the hot chocolate. "See what I mean? Since she's started seeing this Julio, she's suddenly OBSESSED with Spain. I came home the other day to find her watching a Spanish film with the subtitles on."

Even Molly couldn't stay angry in the face of Shenice's worry. "Does she know you know yet?"

"No," Shenice answered glumly. "But I overheard her on the phone saying that she wants to see him twice next week, so it sounds like it's getting serious. If she tries to tell me he's my new dad I promise you I will run away."

It sounded like Shenice's mum was getting on well with this Julio but I knew that wasn't what Shen wanted to hear. "I'm sure she wouldn't do that," I said. "I read this article which said—"

Shenice ignored me. "She talks stupid Spanish all the time. Why else would she do that if not to get me used to the idea of moving to Spain?"

Now SHE looked like she might cry, and I wasn't sure I could handle both my BFFs going supernova at the same time. "You should follow her next time she goes to meet him," I said, pleased that my new journalistic instincts were coming in handy. "See what this Julio dude looks like."

Shenice sipped her hot chocolate thoughtfully.

"You know, that's not a bad idea. But I can't do it on my own." She threw us her best puppy-dog look. "You will both come, won't you?"

Molly and I looked at each other, and I knew we were both wondering how we'd get out of our houses late on a school night. But we'd think of something – Shenice needed us and we'd only be following her mum. What could possibly go wrong?

Possible Articles for the School Paper

THE YEAR SEVEN ITCH
Epidemic of nits in Year Seven (well, three cases, plus
one that was less an infestation and more a fruit fly
having a snooze). Is this a sinister conspiracy by the
school nurse to keep her job? Maybe she has a secret
nit farm under those grey curls.

WHEN GOOD DINNER LADIES GO BAD
Pretty sure the canteen staff are on a secret mission
to kill us through malnutrition. Seriously, the salads
are so slimy they could go on Jeremy Kyle.

CROSS-COUNTRY: IS IT LEGAL?
Of course it isn't. This may be the subject of my
next petition.

BEAUTY TIPS FOR BUSY GIRLS

Might "borrow" some from THE THRIFTY GAL'S GUIDE TO GORGEOUSNESS (although from what Mr Bearman said, this could be plagiarism).

WILLIAM SHAKESPEARE

Am sure I read somewhere that his plays were all written by monkeys with typewriters. Can't believe no one has investigated this.

Not sure about any of these ideas, Cassie. Anything juicier? K xx

CHAPTER SEVEN

DISASTER! Woke up this morning thinking it was Monday
and packed all the books I'd need, only for Liam to
gleefully remind me that it was actually Tuesday – stupid
BANK HOLIDAY MONDAY. After I'd repacked my bag,
Ethel projectile-vomited into my Coco Pops, which put me
off eating **EVER** again, but Mum insisted on making me
some toast, all of which meant I was too late to meet
Molly and Shenice. Thank goodness I washed and blow-
dried my hair last night, which meant it was silky smooth
for once this morning and didn't even needed brushing

– just as well, since I didn't really wake up properly until halfway through registration. That little hair-care tip I picked up from **THE THRIFTY GAL'S GUIDE TO GORGEOUSNESS** has really worked. Mum might not be so impressed when she finds out there are no eggs left in the fridge but my hair feels great. Might try rinsing it with beer next time – am sure Dad won't mind.

It wasn't until maths was nearly over that I noticed Molly and Shenice were whispering to each other and looking at me like I'd grown another head.

"What?" I said, wondering if I'd forgotten to wash the blob of nappy cream off the monster spot I'd felt growing on my chin last night. "Why are you staring at me?"

"It's nothing," Molly replied timidly. "Only... well, we wondered why...is that **SCRAMBLED EGG** in your hair?"

Instantly, my hand flew to my head and my fingers groped around my scalp. Sure enough, there were little bobbles of something there. When I pulled my hand away and inspected under my nails, it looked suspiciously like scrambled egg. I gazed down at it in utter bewilderment. I hadn't even had time to snatch up a slice of toast this morning, let alone a cooked breakfast, so how had I managed to get egg in my hair? Unless...

My eyes widened in panic. I'd rinsed my hair in eggs last night, like THE THRIFTY GAL'S GUIDE TO GORGEOUSNESS suggested. Then I'd blow-dried it. What if I hadn't rinsed the egg away properly? The heat from the hairdryer would have cooked whatever was left, meaning that instead of a glossy mane of hair, I was quite literally an EGGHEAD. I gasped and raised ⟶ my hand.

"Please, sir, can I go to the toilet?"

Mr Peterson didn't even look up. "I'm sure you can wait ten more minutes until break, Cassidy."

I thought about pushing it but people were starting to glance over at me already and I didn't want them looking too closely. Especially not Nathan. So I lowered my hand and casually started to peel the bigger lumps of egg out of my hair and drop them on the floor, wishing that Rolo was there to eat the evidence. There were going to be some very confused cleaners in that classroom at the end of the day.

"How is it looking?" I muttered to Molly and Shenice, who were watching me with expressions of horrified fascination.

"A bit better," Shenice conceded. "A lot less Humpty Dumpty, definitely."

"How did it happen?" Molly asked.

By the time I'd whispered an explanation, in between glares from Mr Peterson, it was the end of the lesson. I stuffed my books into my bag with lightning speed. The sooner I got to the girls' toilets and sorted my head out, the better.

"Uh, Cassie," Molly said, her voice full of warning. "I'm guessing you don't want to talk to Nathan right now? Only he's heading this way."

No, **no, NO,** this could not be happening. I couldn't let him see me like this – he'd think I had the worst case of dandruff ever. Rummaging in my bag, I pulled out my scarf and wrapped it around my head, just as he arrived at our table.

"Oh, hi, Nathan," I said, ignoring the puzzled looks I was getting from the rest of my classmates as they

89

filed out of the room. "How are you?"

His gaze slid to my head. "I'm fine. Why have you got a scarf wrapped around your head?"

I giggled nervously. "It's for the school magazine," I improvised, and next to me, Molly and Shenice nodded feverishly. "I'm doing an article on fashion and thought I'd better test out this season's hot new looks."

"Right," he said slowly. "And that's a hot new look, is it?"

I nodded carefully, trying not to picture lumps of scrambled egg flying off to hit him in the face. "Yeah, didn't you see last month's **VOGUE**?" I said, in a bright, shrill voice. "Everyone in Paris is wearing them. So, what can I do for you?"

He cleared his throat and glanced at Molly and Shenice. "I – uh—"

This was a first – I'd never seen Nathan Crossfield anything other than ice-cool and unless I was wrong, he was nervous about something. Molly and Shenice were staring at him with expectant eyes. I aimed a meaningful look their way. "I'll see you outside, shall I?"

Thankfully, they took the hint. When it was just the two of us, Nathan tried again. "There's a new milkshake place on Peascod Street."

It wasn't quite what I was expecting him to say but I had noticed it. The Sugar Rush Mountain shake sounded like my idea of heaven. "Yeah?"

He gazed at me, his smoky blue eyes serious. "I – uh – wondered if you'd like to go there one day. With me. For a milkshake."

Did he mean as a mate or as – well – more than a mate? I wondered. Then I decided it didn't matter – I'd get to spend some time with him outside of school. "Er, yeah," I said, smiling. "I would."

He smiled back, as though he'd been expecting me to say no. As IF.

"Good. How about Saturday?"

"Okay," I said, trying to keep my smile from morphing into a big goofy grin.

"Alright. Shall I come to your house?"

I tried not to cringe as I remembered the last time he'd been in my house. "As long as you promise not to judge me. Between the twins and Rolo, it's kind of a mess."

"I promise," he said, with a crinkly-eyed smile that made my stomach flip over. "Oh, and Cassie?"

I picked up my bag and headed for the door. "Yes?"

His gaze flickered upwards and he shook his head. "I'm not sure Windsor is hot enough for that look, to be honest."

Feeling my cheeks turn pinker than my scarf, I turned and ran. Straight into Kelly.

"Hi, Cassie," she said, smiling. Then she caught sight of my makeshift hat and her smile faded into a frown. "Everything okay?"

This could not be happening! I couldn't use the same excuse I'd used with Nathan – Kelly might think I was writing for a rival publication. "Erm..."

Her eyes narrowed as she stared at me. "What's going on with your hair?"

My mind raced through the possibilities. What could I tell her that wouldn't result in instant social death? Was temporary leprosy even grosser than the truth?

She leaned closer and pulled the scarf away. "Is it... EGG?"

And that was it – I couldn't lie any more. With a quick glance around to make sure Nathan had gone, I accepted my fate with a groan. "Yes. Yes, it is."

To her credit, Kelly didn't laugh. Instead, she shook her head and linked her arm through mine. "I can't have one of my crew walking around like that," she said. "Why don't you come to the toilets and I'll sort it out for you?"

In a daze, I let her lead me through the corridors.

I mean, I knew she had a reputation as the NICEST
PERSON EVER but this was above and beyond that.
I wouldn't have blamed her for collapsing into hysterical
laughter and here she was helping me out. She really was
an angel sent from above.

The girls' toilets weren't empty when we walked in
but the second Kelly asked for a bit of space, the crowds
around the mirrors melted away.

"That's better," Kelly said, as the door swung shut
and we were alone. "Now, let's see what we can do."

She rummaged in her bag, presumably looking for
a hairbrush. I caught sight of myself in the mirror and
groaned – there were lumps of yellow and white egg
EVERYWHERE and the collar of my blazer was speckled
with blobs too. Seriously, I looked like I'd stepped
straight off a poster for infectious diseases. My cheeks
turned rosy and I closed my eyes in utter mortification.

How do I get myself into these situations? How?

I stood there in silence, wondering if I should try to explain myself. Kelly would understand, wouldn't she? She might even use some of THRIFTY GAL'S tips herself – not the egg one, obviously, but some of the others. Not that Kelly needs beauty tips, of course – she is always perfectly groomed.

Kelly was staring at her phone when I opened my eyes. She dropped it into her bag the moment she saw me watching and pulled out a hairbrush.

"Right," she said, stepping forward with a determined smile. "I'll brush, you talk. How on earth did you get yourself into this mess?"

She was a total superstar. By the time I walked out

of the toilets, my hair was gleaming and my eggy conditioner was nothing more than the kind of memory I might laugh about some day. In a hundred years' time, maybe.

Kelly gave me a friendly smile as I walked into the English block at lunchtime. The usual gang were all there. This time, Mr Bearman had us reviewing previous editions of the magazine, figuring out what had worked and what hadn't. Kieran had his **WOLF BRETHREN** exclusive and it wasn't as cringey as I'd been expecting. It always amazes me when I realize how much people like them. I know Liam is the kind of idiot who makes me smell his farts, whereas the rest of the school see him as the cool lead singer in a pretty good band.

I got my first assignment too, although I was disappointed that they hadn't gone for one of my great article pitches. Instead, Mr Bearman suggested I talk to George Thompson in Year Seven about the recent

Outward Bound trip to Wales, and after a guilty smile as I remembered the sinking raft photos on JOJ, I agreed to do it. As we were leaving, Kelly took me to one side and my heart sank. Don't tell me there was MORE egg to be brushed out?

But it wasn't anything to do with my hair. In fact, she seemed to have forgotten all about it. "How do you like working on HEY JUDE'S! so far?" she asked.

"I love it," I blurted out, then realized how hideously uncool I sounded. "I mean, it's been okay."

Kelly smiled. "Believe me, you're a natural. Don't tell anyone I said this but you're the best new journalist we've ever had."

My heart swelled with pride, even though I wasn't sure how she would know that, given that I hadn't actually covered anything yet. "Really?"

She glanced over her shoulder, as though checking no one was listening in. "Totally. If only the others were half as good as you, then maybe I wouldn't have this problem."

"What problem?" I said, frowning. As far as I could tell, the biggest problem Kelly Anderson had was keeping up with all her Twitter followers. "Is it anything I can help with?"

She leaned closer. "It's nothing, really. I just need some information about this girl in Year Seven for one of my articles and no one seems to know anything."

Here it was, my chance to prove to Kelly I was a good journalist. "Which girl?"

"Hannah de Souza," she replied. "I'm doing a piece about self-confidence and body image and I heard this rumour that Hannah had some kind of plastic surgery.

Only I don't know if it's true."

I'd bet my signed Droids poster it was. Hannah
had gone to Westwood Primary, the same as me and
Molly and Shenice, and she'd always had the mickey
taken out of her for her ears. It wouldn't be a complete
surprise if she'd had them sorted out, although I'd hardly
call it plastic surgery — I mean, it wasn't like she'd had
a nose job or a tummy tuck. But Kelly was biting her lip
in a worried kind of way and I was keen to help if I
could. "I know Hannah," I told her. "Maybe I can ask her
for you."

Kelly beamed at me. "Would you? That would be so
brilliant!" She hesitated and looked thoughtful. "But
maybe you shouldn't tell her I'm interested. I'll make
sure I don't use her real name in my story."

I supposed it made sense. "Okay."

"Excellent," she said, her eyes shining. "I knew I'd made the right choice when I picked you."

She left me standing there, feeling pretty pleased with myself. First Nathan, now this — if I didn't count Egg-gate, today was in the running to be my Best Day Ever!

To: <u>BondGirl007</u>

From: <u>Mariella.Evergreen@WindsorRecorder</u>

Hi Cassidy,

Thanks for your email with suggestions on how we can "sass up" the Windsor Recorder. You have some great ideas – sadly, I don't think the majority of our readers are quite ready to "get with it" but I could be wrong.

While I am impressed to hear that you can complete the Glitz crossword in less than ten minutes, I'm afraid I don't think that is a strong enough basis for you to write a weekly showbiz column for the paper. And although I enjoyed your poem about Rory from The Droids's nose ring, I'm not sure it's quite right for us.

I hope you are not too disappointed by this.

Thanks again for getting in touch and good luck with your journalism career!

Best wishes,

Mariella Evergreen

Commissioning Editor – Windsor Recorder

CHAPTER EIGHT

Molly and Shenice weren't so impressed with my new secret mission.

"Sounds to me like she's got you doing her dirty work," Molly sniffed when I explained on the way home.

"What's dirty about it?" I objected. "Either Hannah's had her ears fixed or she hasn't. Maybe she's really proud of her new streamlined look and is waiting for someone to ask her about it."

Shenice chewed on her Wham bar. "I don't think I'd want everyone to know if I'd had something like that done. It's a bit personal, isn't it?"

I gave up. "What do you think I should wear to meet up with Nathan?"

Molly sniggered. "Not that scarf or the yolk will be on you."

"Eggsactly!" Shenice said, grinning.

"You crack me up," Molly said and they both cackled like they were the FUNNIEST PEOPLE EVER.

"Oh, ha ha," I said. "Please stop, you're making my sides hurt."

Shenice smirked. "Eggscell—"

"Don't," I warned. "Just don't."

We walked along for a while, with the two of them whispering lamer and lamer egg jokes to each other until I'd finally had enough. They were meant to be staying at my house for tea but the way things were going, I'd be packing them off home hungry. "Do you want to see the **WOLF BRETHREN** auditions tonight or not?" I demanded, when they were practically wetting themselves with laughter.

The threat had the desired effect – Molly stopped laughing instantly. "Yes."

I scowled. "Then drop the eggy jokes."

They both nodded like they were wobbly-headed toy dogs. ↗

"And promise you'll help me think

of a way to make Hannah spill the beans about her ears," I went on, deciding I might as well get as much out of these auditions as possible.

Again they nodded.

"Okay then," I said. "But if either of you so much as hints at an egg joke, I'll set Joshua and Ethel on you. And believe me, they come fully loaded."

Most people use their garage to keep their car in — not us. Ours is home to the kind of junk charity shops throw out — my popped spacehopper, an old hamster cage and Dad's much-neglected bike. It's also where WOLF BRETHREN rehearse and Liam was already in the garage when we arrived home, setting up for the auditions. He sneered when he saw me, then he spotted Molly and Shenice and turned it into a smarmy smile.

"Hey, ladies, come to see
the legend of the wolf
being reborn?"

I rolled my eyes. **PUR-LEASE.**
Could he be any more ridiculous? But Molly lapped it up,
as usual, and even Shenice looked half-impressed.

"I hope the guitarists who audition know how lucky
they are," Molly said, and I thought I might actually vom.

"Probably not," Liam said. "But it's like Hendrix
always said, 'many are called but few are chosen'."

"That wasn't Hendrix, you idiot, it was Jesus,"
I snorted. "We studied it in RE last week."

Liam scowled at me. "Doesn't matter, because really
only one will be chosen and as the Mollster there says,
they will be lucky." He fired an imaginary shot at Molly

and blew on his fingers. "Are you sticking around for the auditions, babe?"

Molly beamed at him. "Can we?"

"Of course," he said, reaching down behind an amplifier. "I've even got something for you."

I was actually worried Molly might die from excitement, until I saw what was in Liam's hand – a mug with ROCK STAR emblazoned across it. Molly's smile dipped a bit as she took it.

Liam winked. "Milk and two sugars, please."

Don't tell Liam I said this but the auditions were pretty cool. Nine bass players turned up. Four of them barely knew one end of a guitar from the other, two were reasonable and one reminded me of a Muppet, right

down to his crazy red hair and fixed grin. By the time
the audition ended, it was starting to get dark and there
were only two bassists left.

"Do you think her hair is real?" Molly whispered,
glaring at fifteen-year-old Anjel as she leaned against
the garage wall, chatting with Liam. "They're extensions,
right?"

I studied Anjel's long blonde hair. "Looks pretty real
to me."

Shenice squinted across at them. "Hard to say. She's
really good, though. How are they going to decide who
joins the band?"

The other guitarist, Rhys, was talking to Jordan and
Ben, the two remaining members of WOLF BRETHREN.
"Liam says they'll each have to do a solo and whoever
plays the best one is in."

It didn't take a genius to work out which one Molly preferred.

"Rhys was definitely the best," she said loudly, as Anjel laughed at something Liam had said. "He'd fit right in with the band's image too."

Shenice and I exchanged a look. If Anjel did become WOLF BRETHREN's newest member, she'd better watch her back.

The next bit felt like it happened in slow motion. Mum opened the door to the garage to call Dad through and Rolo squeezed through the gap between the door and her legs. He lolloped enthusiastically over to say hello to everyone. Most people made a fuss of him. Anjel ruffled his ears and even got down on her knees to rub his tummy, which I could tell scored massive points with Liam, if not Molly. Then Rolo romped across to Rhys and things went a bit wrong. In his excitement, Rolo got a bit confused about what the guitar in Rhys's hand was and clamped his teeth around the neck.

"Hey!" Rhys exclaimed and tugged it back. The strings made a funny ZOING sound, which only made Rolo more playful. Before I knew it, they were having a full on tug-of-war with the guitar, and the strings were twanging madly. Everyone was laughing but all I could see was Rhys's face getting redder and redder.

I got up to pull Rolo away but I wasn't quite quick enough. With a shout of annoyance, Rhys yanked the neck out of Rolo's mouth and aimed a kick at his brown tummy. Rolo danced out of the way but the tip of Rhys's trainer still caught him and he let out a startled yelp. The garage fell silent.

Liam stepped forwards, his fists balled into angry fists. "Not cool, man," he said. "Not cool at all."

Rhys started to laugh and then seemed to realize no one else saw the joke. "Stupid dog nearly broke my strings."

I crouched beside a shaking Rolo. "You didn't have to kick him. He'd let go already."

My dad stepped forward and gave the guitar a quick once-over. "I think you'd better leave, young man." He held out a crisp twenty pound note. "This should cover any damage to your strings."

Rhys scowled around the garage. Without a word, he snatched the money out of my dad's hand and stormed off into the twilight.

For a second, nobody spoke. Then Liam turned to Anjel and grinned. "Congratulations, you made the band. When can you start?"

"They're making a huge mistake," Molly fumed, as we sat in my room and waited for her mum to come. "They'll have to change their name for a start."

Shenice looked confused. "Why?"

"Because they can hardly be called WOLF BRETHREN with a girl member, can they?" Molly said, in a slow voice as though Shenice was an idiot. "WOLF SIBLINGS doesn't have quite the same ring, does it?"

"I'm sure they'll figure something out," I said soothingly. "You do want them to play at the May Ball, don't you?"

From the look on Molly's face, it was touch and go. "Yeah, of course."

Oh dear. Anjel has got some serious work to do if she wants to win over **WOLF BRETHREN**'s number-one fan.

It turned out to be the easiest thing ever to find out about Hannah's ears — all I had to do was ask her. She told me she'd had it done the summer after we'd finished primary school but had kept it to herself, hoping to start St Jude's without any jokes. It hadn't even hurt that much, the worst bit had been having to wear a weird Professor Quirrell turban thing to keep her ears flat. I listened, storing up as much detail as I could in my head to pass on to Kelly. And then she said she didn't mind telling me about it because she knew I could be trusted. That's when it all went wrong, because I knew right then that I couldn't tell Kelly anything about Hannah's operation. Feeling a bit sick, I told Hannah how great she looked, and went to find a brick wall to bash my head against.

Sitting on the steps outside the science block,
I gnawed at my fingernails until they were all gone.
I'm just starting to get the hang of journalism – I had
this brilliant idea for a cutting exposé about Mr
Peterson's maths class and I'll be gutted if Kelly kicks
me off the magazine. She's always been lovely to me,
of course, but what if she doesn't understand why Hannah
wants her private life to **STAY** private?
My new career will be over
before it has really begun.

I wonder if it's too late
to join the circus...

I don't know why I was scared about telling Kelly – she
couldn't have been nicer.

"Of course I understand," she reassured me, when I
passed on the bad news about Hannah. "I can totally see

why she wouldn't want her secret splashed all over the magazine."

I heaved a sigh of relief and made a mental note to stick my tongue out at Molly and Shenice. They'd been convinced Kelly would demand that I spilled the beans. And if anything, the fact that she was so lovely made me feel even worse that I couldn't give her the lead she needed.

"I'm really sorry to let you down," I mumbled. "Maybe I'm not cut out to be a journalist after all."

"Rubbish," she replied, with a dismissive shake of her head. "I'll just have to find another example for my story. It's a shame, though. Hannah was a perfect role model to other girls who are unhappy with their looks."

She let out a wistful sigh, making me feel even worse. I hadn't thought of it that way. But Hannah had confided in me, I couldn't betray her, no matter how desperate I was to please Kelly. "Sorry."

She smiled as though it didn't matter at all. "I'll probably shelve the whole article now." There was a brief pause, then she went on, "I'd love to know what she had done, though. I think she's so brave."

I looked sideways at her. Now that I came to think about it, Hannah had been brave. Maybe she'd feel better about it if someone as popular as Kelly was on her side.

"Uh..." I hesitated.

Kelly widened her eyes. "I wouldn't breathe a word to anyone, I swear."

And now I had a major dilemma. On the one hand,

Hannah had trusted me with her secret on the understanding that I wouldn't share it. But on the other hand, I had Kelly, Miss Popularity and the nearest thing I had to a boss, telling me I could trust her. She seemed to genuinely care about Hannah and I wanted her to like me so much it practically hurt. And it wasn't as though Hannah was exactly a BFF – we'd just gone to the same primary school. But deep down, I knew I shouldn't even be thinking about spilling her secret.

"Did I mention I'm having a party in half-term?" Kelly's voice cut casually into my thoughts. "Only my favourite people are invited."

My heart sank further towards my feet. I wasn't one of her favourites – how could I be when I'd failed her? She glanced over. "I think Nathan Crossfield might even be coming. And Susie Carr."

I stared at her for a few seconds, consumed by a

sudden surge of jealousy. If Nathan and Susie were going to the party then I had to be there too: I **HAD** to. And maybe I was making too big a deal out of all of this, anyway. It wasn't as though I was blabbing Hannah's secret all over school – she never needed to know I'd told anyone.

In spite of this logic, it still took almost a minute for me to wrestle my conscience to the ground. "Okay," I said eventually, pushing the last doubts firmly to the back of my mind. "This is for your ears only..."

JUICE ON JUDE'S

LOVE IS IN THE AIR!

WHICH YEAR EIGHT
HOTTIE WAS SPOTTED
LEAVING WHICH YEAR
SEVEN HUNK'S HOUSE
YESTERDAY EVENING?

It seems like Susie Carr has got herself a toy boy in the shape of Nathan Crossfield and JOJ thinks they make such a cute couple. A source close to Nathan said he'd "never been happier". No prizes for guessing who he'll be taking to the May Ball!

← (STUPID SUSIE CARR!)

(STUPID MAY BALL)

WOLVES BITE BACK?

After JOJ exclusively reported that Max Smith was leaving the band, rumours abound of fierce arguments and back-stabbing in the Wolf Brethren pack. It seems Liam's relationship with hot new bass player, Anjel Philips, is causing tensions to run high and the band is on the verge of a major rift. The Brethren are due to thrill the crowds at the May Ball next week – if they last that long...

(Hmmm...Liam hasn't mentioned any arguments and I am pretty sure him and Anjel aren't together. WHO is writing this stuff?)

CHAPTER NINE

OMG to the MAX. You will not believe who Shenice's mum is dating. Seriously, I don't even believe it and I have seen the evidence with my own eyes. I think I may still be in shock.

It is SO much worse than we suspected. I don't know if you've ever followed someone but it is a lot less exciting in real life than it looks on TV. We waited a few minutes after Shenice's mum had gone on Thursday evening, then sneaked out of the back door while her brother was playing **SPECIAL FORCES – VAMPIRE ANNIHILATION** on the XBox. At first, we bobbed in and out of doorways, pretending we were from MI5 (with a name like mine, it is practically the law to imagine you are a spy) but we soon realized Shenice's mum had no idea we were there and started to act a bit more normally.

It didn't stop Shenice from fretting, though. By the time her mum had disappeared into what we assumed was Julio's house, she was all pale and sweaty.

"It doesn't look very Spanish," Molly said, as we stared at the small terraced house with its flower-filled hanging basket and neatly trimmed hedge. ⟶

"Were you expecting a bull in the front garden?"

I shot back, trying to peer through the window. "Or maybe a piñata?"

"I'm just saying it looks like the kind of house someone ordinary might live in," Molly said reasonably, and she threw me a meaningful look. "Someone nice."

"What if that's my future stepdad in there?" Shenice moaned, as a shadow flitted tantalizingly behind the curtains.

It was beginning to dawn on me that we hadn't really thought this through. Now that Shen's mum was inside, we had no real way to spy on her. "Erm, how are we going to see who she's with?"

Shenice and Molly stared at me.

"I hadn't thought of that," Molly admitted.

Suddenly an idea came to me. "Knock Down Ginger?"

As plans went, it wasn't exactly MI5 material but it was the best I could offer at short notice. We didn't have long – Shen's brother was bound to notice we were gone sooner or later and my dad was coming to pick us up from our "homework brainstorming session" at eight o'clock. And nobody had any better ideas.

Molly and Shenice crouched behind a parked car while I crept up the front path. The plan was to sneak up and knock on the door, before running off to hide. But I failed to spot a milk bottle beside the door until it was too late. It clattered to the floor and rolled down the path, rattling all the way. A light snapped on behind the door. I turned and ran, hiding behind the hedge. As the door creaked open, I peered through the leaves. This was it – the moment when I got a glimpse of Shenice's potential future. I blinked, and blinked again, not quite sure if I was really seeing what I thought I was seeing.

Standing on the doorstep, with a half-drunk bottle of beer in his hand, was our Spanish teacher, Mr Ramirez.

I gave a sigh of relief and crept back to the girls. "It's okay, she's not with Julio," I told them, grinning. "She's with Mr Ramirez from school."

Shenice let out a horrified wail and Molly stared at me, stony-faced, until the penny dropped. I gasped and my eyes widened. "Oh, oh, I bet his name is Julio." My hands flew to my face. "Shenice, your mum is dating Mr Ramirez!"

Molly held an imaginary microphone to her lips. "This just in from the Minister for the Completely Obvious."

"I want to go home," Shenice puffed, so pale that I didn't know if she would puke or pass out first. "Please, just take me home."

We didn't talk much on the way back and even now, three hours later, I'm still in shock. I mean, Mr Ramirez is really nice but it's a ginormous no-no for your parents to date a teacher. If this gets out, Shenice is going to DIE.

And I thought I had problems...

Mum's voice turned my blood to ice as it floated up the stairs on Saturday afternoon.

"It's Nathan, isn't it?"

Nathan was already sitting on the sofa when I hurtled down the stairs two at a time before she did something embarrassing, like breathing. Right now she was swaying in the middle of the living room, a twin perched on each hip. I'd noticed the sway was pretty much a permanent thing these days, even when the twins were fast asleep in their cots.

"Yeah," Nathan said, nodding. Mum looked ridiculously pleased with herself, like she'd just discovered the secret of eternal life or something. I don't see how she can remember the name of someone who's been to our house once but forgets to take the keys out of the front door when she comes in. Her baby brain seems to be a permanent thing now.

"Hi," I said breathlessly.

"Hey," he replied and cleared his throat. "I'd stand up but your dog is sitting on my foot."

I looked down. Sure enough, Rolo was glued to Nathan's trainer, globules of stringy slobber hanging out of his mouth as he gazed up, panting.

"Er, this might seem like an odd question but have you got cheese in your pocket?" I asked.

To his credit, Nathan didn't seem to think I'd lost the plot. "No, but I did have cheese on toast for breakfast this morning."

That explained it — Rolo is to cheese what sniffer dogs are to drugs. If cheddar ever gets made illegal, he will have a whole new career ahead of him. They will call him THE NOSE and he will have his own television show called CHEESE QUEST. And I will be his patient yet doting owner.

"It's his cheese radar," I told Nathan. "Our next-door neighbours only have to get their grater out and he tries to climb through their cat flap."

"Right, no cheese for twenty-four hours before I visit next time," he said gravely and I liked him a little bit more.

Mum coughed, as though reminding us that she was there.

"We should get going," I said, pulling on my coat. My hand hovered over my scarf and out of the corner of my eye, I saw Nathan grin. Maybe I'd brave the weather without it.

"Have fun," Mum called. "Be good!"

I slammed the front door fast before she could come out with any more Mum-isms. I'm pretty sure they go to a special school to learn how to be embarrassing at all times. I explained my theory to Nathan, as we headed down the road to the town centre.

"Mine is the same," he agreed. We walked in silence for a moment. "Your little brother and sister are cute."

I grimaced. "You wouldn't say that if you met them

at three in the
morning.
They morph
into monsters
during the night."

We chatted all the way to the town centre. I was
dying to ask about him and Susie but I couldn't think of
a way to slip it into the conversation without sounding
like a mad stalker girl, and by the time we reached The
Shake Shack, he'd distracted me so much that I'd almost
forgotten. It was busy but we managed to squeeze
around a table in the corner. I couldn't decide what was
better, being on a non-date with Nathan, or being in a
place where Oreo cookies and Maltesers were mixed
together in one divine drink.

"How's the magazine stuff going?" Nathan asked
once we'd ordered. "Is it like you expected it to be?"

I hesitated. Part of me wanted to confess that I found being a journalist a bit harder than I'd expected. The ideas I had seemed good, until I started writing them down and then it all went wrong. My assignment about the Year Seven Outward Bound trip was due in soon and I couldn't work out whether to make it serious or jokey. But journalism was supposed to be my THING — I couldn't admit that I was struggling to anyone and I definitely couldn't ask for help. So I plastered on a big breezy smile. "It's amazing. Everyone is really nice. How's being on the School Council? Is it like being a Member of Parliament?"

"It would be if the main business of Parliament was deciding how many water coolers we need and where to put them," he replied, pulling a face. "You wouldn't believe how many arguments that caused."

I'd watched a bit of Prime Minister's Questions on one of the satellite channels one afternoon, not long after my petition had started to get really popular, and it had been the most boring thing ever – just a load of grumpy old men mumbling away and a bossy voice shouting "Order! ORDER!" all the time. I don't know where all the waiters were but some of the MPs had fallen asleep.

"If my petition gets enough signatures, it might be debated in Parliament," I told Nathan, thinking that the idea had lost some of its shine now I knew that our MPs' idea of debate was muttering incoherently until the opposition nodded off.

But Nathan seemed enthusiastic. "Yeah, nice work on that. I passed the link on to all my mates and they all signed it."

My ears went hot as I blushed – Nathan was telling his friends about me! Well, okay, it was really the petition he was talking about, but still! "Thanks," I said, suddenly shy.

"No problem," he replied. "Listen, I'm sorry we haven't seen each other much since the quiz team broke up. I kind of miss those cramming sessions we used to have."

Did that mean he missed me as well? Or had he meant the team as a whole? It was probably a good thing our milkshakes arrived right then or I might have gushed how much I missed him too. As it was, I was awed into silence by my **SUGAR RUSH MOUNTAIN**. It was every bit as gorgeous as the description suggested – I could practically feel my teeth rot just looking at it.

"There was another reason I asked you here today," Nathan said, after a few minutes' industrious spoon-work, and I realized he suddenly looked even more nervous than he had on Thursday. "I – er – wondered if you – uh – wanted to go to the May Ball."

Duh. Of course I did. "Yeah," I replied, frowning. "Everyone is going, aren't they?"

He flashed a frozen smile. "I meant with me."

"Oh," I said and felt my cheeks start to go red. "OH!"

The headline from **JOJ** loomed large in my mind. How could he be asking me if he was already going with Susie? "Um...won't your girlfriend be upset?"

His mouth dropped open. "My girlfriend?"

Nervously, I fiddled with my straw. "I thought you'd be going with Susie Carr. Only it said on **JUICE ON JUDE'S** that she'd been to your house and everyone had kind of put two and two together..."

I trailed off uncertainly as a flicker of irritation crossed his face.

"You shouldn't believe everything you read on JOJ," he said, in a grim tone. "My mum is Susie's piano teacher, so she comes round to my house once a week for lessons. That doesn't make her my girlfriend."

I looked down at the table, wishing I'd kept my stupid mouth shut. Of course there was nothing going on with Susie. "Sorry."

As the strained silence stretched, I thought about asking if Nathan knew who was behind JUICE ON JUDE'S but then his fingers touched mine and I forgot the website even existed. "There's only one girl I want to go to the ball with," he said quietly, "and she's sitting right here."

A warm fuzzy feeling flowed through me as my eyes met his and all thoughts of Susie flew out of my head. "Really?"

He grinned. "Really. So what do you think?"

I squashed the urge to leap up and squeal with happiness. "I'd love to."

I'm not one hundred per cent sure how I got home from Shake Shack. I think maybe Dad picked me up but I was so busy floating in a bubble of May Ball bliss that I might have pranced home on a purple pony for all I remember. I know I texted Molly and Shenice and I could practically hear their shrieks from the middle of town. We all agreed that I need to start thinking about what I am going to wear. Now that I am going with Nathan, I will definitely need a new dress and there are less than seven days to find one.

I wonder how much my MOSHI MONSTERS would get on eBay?

Sample article for HEY JUDE'S!

DULLEST TEACHER EVER?

Ask any St Jude's student who
their favourite teacher is and
they'll probably take a moment to
think. But ask them who the dullest teacher at
St Jude's is and they won't hesitate: Mr Peterson. And
his double maths lessons are enough to drive terror
into the hearts of all but the geekiest students. One
boy, who didn't want to be named, said, "Mr Peterson
should make one of them apps for people with
insomnia, because he definitely sends me to sleep."

$$a = 1 \pm \frac{\sqrt{14}}{2}$$

$$(a-1) = \pm \frac{\sqrt{14}}{2}$$

$$a = \frac{2}{2} - \frac{\sqrt{14}}{2}$$

But the Headteacher seems oblivious to the problem, in spite of three cases of students falling off chairs in Mr Peterson's lessons in the last week alone. There's no medical evidence but this journalist is convinced there's a connection between the teacher's extreme snoresomeness and the rocketing injury rate.

Cassie, please see me about this.

Mr Bearman

CHAPTER TEN

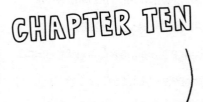

Catching Mum in a good mood is as tricky as trying to get Batman and Bruce Wayne in the same room. But if I wanted a new outfit for the ball, I had to start dropping hints. I thought about hitting her with some really bad news, like I'd been excluded from school, and then following it up with an "Only joking! I do need a new dress, though..." but I doubted she'd be able to hear me with her head in the roof.

In the end, she gave me a gift-wrapped opportunity

at dinner that Saturday night. Miracle of miracles, we'd been allowed to order takeaway pizza and the twins were catnapping in their cot upstairs. The television was on but might as well have been off, since the volume was so low I could barely hear it, and no one was allowed to speak in anything louder than a whisper. Dad was busy trying to convince Liam to do an Elvis cover at the May Ball and Liam was doing his best to pretend that he couldn't hear him.

Mum leaned towards me, her eyes brighter than I'd seen them for ages. "So, Nathan seems nice."

I saw this picture once of a painting called The Scream, →
which is basically someone looking like they've just heard The Droids are splitting up. That's exactly how I felt when Mum winked at me. But I didn't

let her see that she'd got to me. "I'm glad you like him because he's asked me to the May Ball. How amazing is that?"

In a flash, her smile turned into a frown. "I think you're a bit young to be going to parties with boys."

I couldn't believe what I was hearing. When will she stop treating me like a baby? "It's a school party, Mum. All the teachers will be there. And Liam."

Liam stopped stuffing pizza into his face to glare at me. "Don't drag me into it. I'll be too busy being a rock legend to babysit you."

"But you can keep an eye on me, right? To put Mum's mind at rest?" I said, in a wheedling voice, praying that just this once, he might actually do me a favour.

His eyes narrowed and I knew – just KNEW – he was

143

calculating exactly how much mileage he could extract from the situation. "Yeah, I suppose I could do that."

I exhaled very quietly and tried not to think about how many cups of tea I was going to have to make him to repay the debt. My gaze slid hopefully to Mum. "So?"

She glanced over at Dad and they had some kind of weird telepathic conversation. I held my breath until she nodded. "Okay, you can go with Nathan. As long as you remember Liam is in charge."

Phase One – complete. Commencing Phase Two. I took another deep breath. "The other thing is, it's sort of a formal party and I don't think I have the right kind of dress."

Mum's lips tightened. "Cassidy, we've been over this.

As much as I hate sounding like a stuck record, we cannot afford to buy you clothes whenever you want them, especially a new dress you'll probably only wear once."

"I won't only wear it once," I protested. "I'll wear it all the time. I'll wear it to bed if it'll make you happy."

"What would make me happy is if both of you understood that we have another two mouths to feed these days and money is not something that grows on trees," she snapped.

I started to say that I was only too aware that there were another two mouths in the house, since the screams they made woke me up every night, but Liam cut me off.

"Don't have a go at me," he said to Mum, sounding wounded. "I don't need a new dress to impress my boyfriend!"

"Who asked you?" I retorted.

And he might have ended up wearing the remains of the deep pan Meat Feast if a thin, reedy wail hadn't floated over the baby monitor and interrupted us, just as my fingers were reaching for the crust.

Mum slumped back on the sofa, looking like she was about to cry, and all at once I felt horrible. Of course I shouldn't be demanding new dresses when we could only just afford to pay the bills. And I should stop looking for ways to get out of our trip to **UNHAPPY SANDS** – Mum and Dad deserved a break too. "You stay there, love," Dad said, waving at Mum. "Cassie will give me a hand, won't you?"

Nodding, I got to my feet and followed him up the stairs. I waited for the inevitable telling-off as we soothed Joshua and Ethel back to sleep. It didn't come. Instead, Dad waited until we'd tiptoed out of the room to press two ten pound notes into my hand.

"Don't tell your mum," he whispered with a smile.

I stared down at the money, remembering Mum's stressed-out face, and handed it back to him. "It's okay. I'm sure I've got something I can wear."

He closed my fingers over the notes. "Don't be daft. We can't have you going to the ball looking like Cinderella's skint sister, can we?"

I smiled gratefully. "Thanks, Dad."

He winked back. "My pleasure. And remember, not a word to Mum. I'll tell her when she's calmed down a bit. Next year, probably."

Mum must have got more sleep than me because on Sunday morning, she greeted me with a big hug and an envelope with twenty pounds in it.

"What's this?" I asked slowly.

"Money for a new dress, silly," she said, sounding so cheerful that I wondered if she'd had a personality transplant overnight. "I hope it's enough. We can't really spare more."

I thought of the money Dad had given me last night, nestled in the drawer of my dressing table and felt a bit sick. "I didn't think we could spare ANY."

Mum adjusted the strap of Joshua's baby rocker and smoothed down the tuft of hair at the front of his head. "I know the last few months have been tough on you, Cassie, so I borrowed it from the holiday fund. We don't want you to wear the wrong thing, do we?"

I shook my head. "Mum—"

"No arguments," she said firmly. "Go shopping with Molly and Shenice and get something nice. Just don't tell your dad."

I don't know about you but I did not see this coming. Dad has given me money with instructions not to tell Mum. And now Mum has given me money with instructions not to tell Dad. Am I supposed to spend all of it, some of it or none of it? Is it some kind of test?

I bet Taylor Swift never has this problem.

WAILS IN WALES
by Cassidy Bond

St Jude's students were forced to live like cavemen on a recent Outward Bound trip to Wales, an insider says. Supposedly there to learn "teambuilding skills" and join in "healthy exercise", Year Seven students found themselves up to their armpits in water when a raft-building exercise went badly wrong.

LOGS
One traumatized victim, who did not want to be named, said, "We could have drowned. All we had were three soggy logs and some rope and they expected us to stay afloat! It was like my worst nightmares, only wetter."

BEANS

Even George Thompson, a seasoned camper and Outward Bounder, was shocked at the minimalist rations. "The food was pretty basic," he said. "Sharing a dormitory with seven other boys is bad enough but it's much worse when you've all had beans for tea every night."

BUSHES

He went on, "One day, we had to climb up this

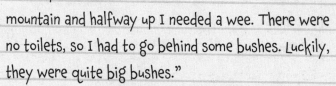

mountain and halfway up I needed a wee. There were no toilets, so I had to go behind some bushes. Luckily, they were quite big bushes."

Cassie, please can we have a chat about this?
I think it needs more work. Mr Bearman

CHAPTER ELEVEN

Nathan gave me the sweetest smile in registration today.
I'm still not one hundred per cent convinced that I didn't
dream the whole weekend but it does appear that Nathan
asked me to the May Ball and that my parents
inadvertently gave me forty pounds to buy something to
wear, which kind of took the edge off the discovery that
Rolo had peed on my rug this morning.

At break, Molly and Shenice were desperate to hear
every last detail about how Nathan had popped the question.

"Did he write it on a note and tie it to a balloon? Or did he spell it out in those candy letters you can buy?" Molly asked, with a faraway look in her eyes, as though she was picturing the scene. "Ooh, did he get down on one knee?"

Shenice and I looked at each other, both wondering what planet she was actually on.

"Calm down, Molly," Shenice said, shaking her head. "He asked her to the ball, not to get married."

Molly looked embarrassed. "Yeah, sorry. It's just that if Liam ever asked me out, I like to think that's how he'd do it."

I laughed. The truth is Liam is about as romantic as ringworm, which made it even more unlikely that he'd made a move on Anjel, now I came to think about it. Whoever was behind JOJ, they'd got that completely

wrong. "Speaking of romance," I said, turning
to Shenice, "any sign that your mum is
planning to tell you about her and SEÑOR AMOR?"

She shuddered and glanced around to make sure no
one could overhear us. "No, but he did say BUENOS DIAS
when he passed me in the corridor this morning."

Molly eyed her sympathetically. "Ah. He's being all
friendly so that it won't be such a shock when he marries
your mum." Her eyes drifted away again. "I wonder how
he'll propose."

"I can't believe this is happening!" Shenice blurted
out, stamping her foot angrily and causing several people
to stop what they were doing to stare at her. "I don't
want a stepdad!"

And she especially didn't want one who worked at
the school. "Have you – er – thought about asking your

mum what's going on?" I asked. "There might be a reasonable explanation."

She rounded on me. "Oh yeah, I'm sure there's a good reason why she's spending so much time with our Spanish teacher."

Several more heads turned our way. "Ssshh!" I hissed. If Shenice wasn't careful, the whole school was going to know about her mum and Mr Ramirez and she'd ~~HAVE~~ to emigrate to Spain to get away from the teasing. "Take it easy, Shen."

Molly joined in and between us, we managed to talk Shenice down from committing social suicide right there in the playground. I don't know how we'll do it next time – she's got the wild-eyed look of a girl totally on the edge.

155

The magazine meeting wasn't as much fun as usual at lunchtime. Mr Bearman asked me how my article was going and I couldn't quite look him in the eye when I said it was coming along. I am determined to get it right on my own, though.

Kelly had another MISSION: IMPOSSIBLE for me after the meeting. At first, I thought she knew I'd lied to Mr Bearman but it turns out she needs to know if it's true that Rachel Muamba got caught smoking by Mrs Pitt-Rivers. She said it's for an article about the dangers of smoking and anything I report back will be completely confidential. I don't know how she expects me to find out – Rachel isn't in my year and I hardly even know her. Her brother is a roadie for WOLF BRETHREN so I suppose I could ask Liam, but the thought of owing him ANOTHER favour makes my teeth hurt. And just like Hannah, I wasn't at all sure Rachel would want anyone to know the truth.

But I didn't say any of that. Instead, I just nodded. That was when she asked if I'd heard any rumours about Mr Ramirez. I swear I nearly swallowed my tongue.

"Mr who?" I repeated thickly, partly because I was trying not to choke and partly to buy my stunned brain some thinking time.

"Mr Ramirez, the Spanish teacher," she said, watching me like Rolo watches next-door's cat. "I heard he's been getting up close and personal with someone's mum."

I wish I could say I came up with something clever to throw her off the scent but my mind had turned to mush. "Oh?" I replied, looking as innocent as I could under the weight of my crushing secret. "Whose parent?"

Her eyes bored into me. "Someone in your year. Do you know anything about that?"

It occurred to me to wonder why she needed to know but I didn't trust myself to ask and Shenice would kill me if I gave the game away. I looked Kelly straight in the eye. "No," I lied.

Kelly stared at me for a few more seconds, then smiled as though we were the best of friends again. "Well, keep your ears open, yeah?" she asked. "I can't use a journalist who doesn't bring me stories, now can I? And I'd hate to leave you off the guest list for my party."

I walked away, shivering. I am beginning to wonder if there is a side to Kelly that no one else sees. Maybe she's not quite as nice as everyone thinks.

Dear Miss Bond,

Thank you for your enquiry about the Golden Nib Journalism Award, given each year for outstanding newspaper writing. I am afraid that your whistle-blowing article entitled *St Jude's: The Hidden Cost of Zzzzzz Lessons,* while interesting and illuminating, is not eligible for this year's award as it was not published in a United Kingdom newspaper in the past twelve months.

However, I have passed your article around many of my colleagues and we all felt that you captured the "extreme snoresomeness" of Mr Peterson's double maths lessons and the difficulties it causes your fellow pupils very well, and your writing certainly entertained us. We wish you lots of luck with your future career.

Yours faithfully,
Seb Gregory
Administrator,
The Golden Nib

CHAPTER TWELVE

School was kind of weird today. The playground was buzzing with whispered conversations but I didn't think anything of it until I noticed people stop talking to stare at me when we were walking past. By the time we'd reached registration, Molly and Shenice had noticed it too and it wasn't only my year group – it felt like kids I didn't even know were talking about me and at break, one boy shouted "Nice hair!" and practically peed his pants with laughter, which was strange because I only had it tied back in a ponytail. Maybe this is what it's like

160

to be famous. I might ask Liam if this kind of thing happens to him.

I don't know whether it is the guilt of knowing that we can't afford the money Mum and Dad gave me to get a dress, or whether Windsor really is the TOWN THAT FASHION FORGOT, but I couldn't find a single thing to buy when I dragged Molly and Shen shopping after school.

Dejected, we trudged into the Shake Shack and ordered a TUTTI FRUTTI SUPREME to share.

"What am I going to do?" I wailed. "The ball is in three days. At this rate, I'll be going in my school uniform."

Molly slurped on her straw. "You know, if you really can't find anything, I might have a dress you can borrow."

I eyed her suspiciously. Molly was known to have an unquenchable obsession with all things pink and frilly. "Why aren't you wearing it?"

"I've already worn it, to my auntie's wedding," she explained. "I was their bridesmaid at Easter, wasn't I?"

"Erm..." I began, trying to remember which auntie had got married. At least one of them has really bad taste in clothes and the last thing I wanted to wear to the ball was a dress with a skirt the size of the moon.

Shenice gave up trying to suck a chunk of frozen strawberry through her straw and picked up a spoon.

"I've seen the pictures. Don't worry, it's not pink.
Or frilly."

"Nah, it's not really my style at all," Molly said.
"You might like it, though."

There was no way I was committing to wearing
something I hadn't seen, no matter how much Shenice
bigged it up, so we finished our shake and headed to
Molly's. We walked slowly, talking about the ball and ways
to bring the wow to the dance floor, but I couldn't help
noticing that Molly grew quieter and quieter, especially
when WOLF BRETHREN were mentioned. Eventually,
I stopped walking and grabbed her arm.

"Okay, Molly, what's up?"

"Nothing," she mumbled, shaking off my hand and
carrying on along the road. "I wish the band was how it
used to be, that's all."

I pursed my lips, thinking back to the rehearsal I'd heard thumping through the garage wall the night before. "They sound pretty good, or as good as CAT FLAPPED ever sounds. I'm hoping Anjel will do something about their lyrics."

Scowling, she kicked at a stone lying on the floor. "Stupid Anjel and her rubbish playing."

I saw Shenice widen her eyes. "That's not really fair—"

Molly rounded on her. "No, I'll tell you what's not fair. It's not fair that Max has quit the band. It's not fair that Anjel is ruining everything – you've seen JUICE ON JUDE'S. It says WOLF BRETHREN are having ARTISTIC DIFFERENCES and everyone knows that means girl trouble." Her lower lip wobbled alarmingly. "And most of all, it's not fair that Liam doesn't remember who I am any more!"

If we weren't careful, she was going to launch a full-scale Molly strop.

"Of course he knows who you are," I soothed. "How could he forget you after everything you've done for them? And if it helps, I don't think he's exactly over the moon with all the stuff that's been on JOJ."

She sniffed and looked hopeful. "Really? Then there's nothing going on between them?"

The warning signs couldn't have been more obvious if they'd danced up and down the road shouting "Ooh, look at me!" – Molly's crush  was reaching epidemic levels. I put on my most reassuring smile. "I'm pretty sure they're just band mates."

I thought back to what Nathan had said to me at the weekend and frowned uneasily. "Maybe we should stop believing everything we see on JUICE ON JUDE'S, anyway."

"Hmm," Molly said, apparently unconvinced. "See what you can find out from him tonight."

What else could I do? Exchanging a helpless look with Shenice, I nodded.

Molly folded her arms in satisfaction. "And drop my name into the conversation, in case he really has forgotten who I am."

Oh yeah. She's got it bad.

O to the M to gobsmacking G, Molly's bridesmaid's dress is perfect. It is sky blue, with silver sequinned straps and

a shimmery blue gauzy layer
which reaches all the way down
to my ankles. It must have been
one of her younger aunties who
got married because it is so
gorgeous I can't even describe
it properly. Mum's face went
all gooey when I modelled it
at home and Dad looked
like he was going to
burst with pride. Liam,
on the other hand, told me
I looked like the runner-up in a MISS UGLY beauty
pageant. Have I mentioned how much I hate him?

Mum left Dad in charge of the twins and followed me
up to my room. I thought she was going to tell me to tidy
it up – little does she know I am treating the floor as my
floordrobe to hide the fact that I accidentally Superglued
a bottle of nail varnish to my butterfly rug.

"Did you have enough money?" she asked, hovering in the doorway as I pretended to pick things up.

I explained. She gave me the hardest squeeze when I handed her the envelope with all of her money still inside. That's when I knew that borrowing Molly's dress had been the right thing to do. Liam might accuse me of being selfish sometimes, and yeah, okay, sometimes he might even be a teensy bit right, but this time I was happy to prove him wrong. All I had to do now was return the rest of the money to Dad and everything would be peachy in Bond HQ. I'll do it tonight, then polish my halo. Who knew being selfless was such fun?

I cannot believe what I have just seen. Remembering my promise to Molly, I went to ask Liam what was going on with him and Anjel and he gave me a really peculiar look and asked if I'd seen JUICE ON JUDE'S.

"Not since Saturday morning," I said. "Why, is there more stuff about you and Anjel?"

He shook his head and threw me a look that was 25% sympathy and 75% disgust. "No. You're the star of the show tonight."

A weird sort of buzzing started in my ears. "What do you mean?"

Spinning the laptop around, he pointed at the screen. "If I hadn't already told everyone you're adopted, I would now."

Squinting, I read the latest headline and my heart started to pound. "EGGHEAD!" it screamed, and below it was a picture of me in my scarf. "WHAT IS CASSIDY BOND COVERING UP?" it read. "A DIY DYE JOB GONE WRONG OR THE WORST CASE OF NITS ST JUDE'S HAS EVER SEEN?" And that wasn't all. Underneath that was a close-up of the back of my hair in all its omeletty glory.

"CASSIE SEEMS TO BE TAKING CHEAP BEAUTY TREATMENTS TO A NEW LOW WITH THIS MESS OF A HAIRSTYLE," it went on. "CAN'T SHE AFFORD PROPER CONDITIONER? IF SHE'S TRYING TO BE A COOL CHICK, SHE'S FAILED — THIS IS ONE BEAUTY TIP NONE OF US WILL BE SCRAMBLING TO COPY!"

For the longest moment, I couldn't breathe. How had this happened? The only people who knew about it were Molly and Shenice and they wouldn't have breathed a word to anyone. And why had it taken a week to appear on the site? There'd been no shortage of stories on there so I supposed I'd had to wait for my turn but still...

Sucking in a deep breath, I thought back to the week before, wondering how anyone could have taken a picture.

Whoever it was must have snapped the close-up while I was in the playground at the start of the day, and the scarf shot soon after, before I'd gone to the bathroom with Kelly to sort it out properly.

The room started to spin.

Kelly.

Feeling dizzy, I shut my eyes and thought hard. She'd had the opportunity to take the close-up, when she'd been supposedly helping me. What if she hadn't been helping me at all? What if she'd been setting me up?

Opening my eyes, I shook the thought away. It couldn't be her — she was far too nice to be responsible for something so nasty. An image of her expression when she'd asked about Mr Ramirez appeared in my mind. She was nice. Wasn't she?

Feeling as though I might throw up all over Liam's messy bedroom floor, I cleared my throat and tried to sound casual. "What else is on there?"

"The usual made-up rubbish," he said, scrolling past a photo of **WOLF BRETHREN** with a great jagged crack down the middle. Then I saw something that almost stopped my heart. There, on the screen, was a scathing post about Hannah de Souza's ear operation, complete with a picture of Dumbo. I felt the colour drain out of my face. "Oh no..."

"Someone you know?" Liam asked.

"Er, yeah. Can I have a look?"

He pushed the laptop towards me. "There you go. Knock yourself out."

I felt him watching me as I sat on the bed. The story had gone up late last night, which was why Molly and Shenice hadn't seen it, and it was stomach-turningly vicious. It was all there, every last detail I'd innocently given to Kelly. And what was even worse was that people had added comments, horrible things they'd never dare to say to Hannah's face. I shut the lid of the laptop and tried not to cry. It had to be Kelly — no one else could have included the bit about Hannah's turban making her feel like Professor Quirrell, the bit that Hannah had told me in confidence and I'd passed straight on to Kelly. It didn't matter that I'd thought I could trust her — I was pretty sure that wouldn't make Hannah feel any better.

Without a word to Liam, I got up and stumbled along the landing to my room. My phone showed six missed calls from Molly and five from Shenice. We met online and our emergency talks lasted for over an hour. They agreed that Kelly must be the brains behind JUICE ON JUDE'S, although I'm not so sure she didn't have help. Looking back, Jimmy had been really shifty at the first magazine meeting, maybe he'd been working on the JUICE ON JUDE'S site then.

And if he's involved...how many of the others are digging out people's secrets and reporting them back to Kelly?

The worst thing is that I can't tell anyone about any of this without incriminating myself. What am I going to do when Hannah finds out what I've done? She's going to kill me and I totally deserve it.

Joining the circus looks pretty good right now.

CHAPTER THIRTEEN

I don't know how Kelly Anderson sleeps at night. I lay awake until the early hours and for once it had nothing to do with Joshua and Ethel — the headlines from JOJ just kept playing over and over in my mind. I didn't know what Hannah would do when she found out I'd betrayed her but she'd be devastated that everyone knew her secret. When I finally did nod off, I dreamed that she told Mrs Pitt-Rivers I had ruined her life and I ended up in prison.

I'm not really sure how I got through the day, to be honest – it felt as though everyone was whispering and pointing at me. It was actually a relief to come home and play peek-a-boo with Ethel and Joshua, who might dribble on me and bite my fingers but who weren't twisting my words for their own entertainment. Mum knew something was wrong, I could feel her watching me at teatime as I pushed my food around the plate, so I made an excuse and escaped upstairs before she started asking questions.

Rolo seemed to sense I was down because he lay at my feet even though I didn't have any cheese on me. I rubbed his soft ears and half-heartedly tried to concentrate on my fractions homework, then my phone flashed up a message. I glanced at the screen – it was from Molly.

Have you seen JOJ?

No OMG. No exclamation marks. No kisses. A worm
of nervousness crawled through me. What now?

No, I typed. *Do I need to look? xx*

Within seconds, my phone pinged again. *Ask Shenice.*

Gnawing my lip, I got up and went to see Liam. He
was lying on his bed, white headphones plugged into the
laptop. There was no point asking him if he'd checked
JOJ – he was still sulking over all the negative WOLF
BRETHREN coverage.

He yanked one earbud out of his ear and the tinny
screech of guitars filled the air. "Haven't you ever heard
of knocking?"

"Never mind that, I need
the laptop." ⟶

"What's the magic word?" he said, placing a hand on the top of the screen. "If you get it wrong, you have to bring me a cup of tea every morning for a week."

My nerves were jangling – I didn't have time for his stupid games. Snatching the laptop away from him, I typed in the JUICE ON JUDE'S address with shaking fingers. Downstairs, I heard the faint ring of the doorbell and ignored it. I had far more urgent things on my mind. Why hadn't Molly just told me what it said? I wondered, as I waited for the JOJ logo to load. What had Kelly done now?

"Cassie?" Mum's voice floated up the stairs. "Shenice is at the door."

I frowned. What in the name of Twiglets was she doing here? And why wasn't this stupid page loading?

"Tell her to come up," I yelled down to Mum.

"Oh no," Liam said, folding his arms. "I'm not having you two giggling and talking rubbish when I'm trying to work on my music. Go back to your own room."

I ignored him and stared at the blank screen, listening for the thud of Shenice's feet on the stairs. It didn't come. Instead, Mum shouted up again and she sounded annoyed. "She doesn't want to. Come down here and speak to her yourself, please."

Letting out a growl of frustration, I whirled around and headed for the stairs. "Don't touch that laptop," I instructed.

Shen had her back to the door when I arrived. "What's up?" I asked. "Your internet isn't broken as well, is it?"

"What's up?" she said loudly, spinning around so that I could see her face was wet with tears. "Well, let's see

– could it have something to do with the fact that my so-called best friend has totally ruined my life?"

My mouth fell open. Who was she on about – Molly?

"Don't act like you don't know what I mean," she went on, her face twisted with anger. "How long did you wait before you went running to tell Kelly? A whole day or did you text her the same night?"

"Shenice, I really don't know—" I began, then trailed off as a horrific suspicion dawned on me.

"Save it, Cassidy," she hissed. "I hope you're happy with your spiteful new friends, because guess what? I'm never speaking to you again!"

She strode off down the path without a single backward glance. In shock, I closed the door and

turned back into the hallway, only to see Liam walking
down the stairs, the laptop in his hands.

"I'm not surprised she's upset," he said, turning
it round to show me a photoshopped image of Shenice
being bottle-fed by Mr Ramirez. "Cassidy Bond, what
have you done?"

Reasons To Be Cheerful

None.

Zero.

Nada.

Shenice thinks I betrayed her, Molly doesn't know what to think and I am beginning to wonder if I did let something slip to Kelly.

Either way, I can't do anything to make it right.

Being a reporter isn't like I thought it would be.

Not sure it's my Thing after all.

WORST.

DAY.

EVER.

CHAPTER FOURTEEN

Shenice is refusing to acknowledge I exist, Molly can't decide if she believes me or not and every time I started to forget how miserable I was, I heard someone else sniggering about Mr Ramirez and Shenice's mum. It sucks to be me so I can only imagine how much suckier it is to be Shen.

I couldn't blame Molly for spending every break and all lunchtime with Shenice. But it meant I was left on my own and it didn't seem fair. We should be working up to fever pitch discussing the ball tomorrow night. Instead, we weren't talking at all and if I hadn't already agreed to go with Nathan, I doubted I'd even be going. I caught him glancing over a few times during the day, a puzzled look on his face when he saw the permafrost between Shenice and me. I'd better explain tomorrow.

Mum must have worked out something was up because she tried to ask if everything was okay. It was just me and her; Dad was out doing an Elvis gig, Liam was putting in one final **WOLF BRETHREN** rehearsal and the twins were asleep. We were sitting with a tub of ice cream between us and the TV on low when she turned to me, a gently concerned expression on her face.

"Did I hear you and Shenice arguing yesterday? Is everything okay?"

For a moment, I was tempted to spill out the whole sorry story – how stupid I'd been in trusting Kelly – and let Mum cuddle me until it felt better. But I couldn't face seeing the disappointment in her eyes when she realized I'd messed up again. So I summoned up a false smile and lied through my teeth.

"Oh yeah. It was all a big misunderstanding. We're good now."

She studied me for a moment. "You know I'm always here for you, don't you? Even if my eyes are sometimes propped up with matchsticks and I've got my T-shirt on inside out?"

This time my smile was genuine. "Yeah."

She turned back to the TV. "Good."

She dozed off not long after that and I sat staring

at the tiny figures on the screen without really
noticing what they were doing. Shenice and Molly and
me have fallen out before, of course, but it's always
been over stupid stuff and we've made up eventually.
The way Shenice had looked at me yesterday, like I'd
stabbed her through the heart with a rusty knitting
needle, had been different, though. I wasn't sure if I
could **EVER** make it up to her. What if she feels the same
and we **NEVER** make up? How will I cope if I lose my
besties for good?

I am trying my hardest to get into the party spirit but,
after another day in the friendship-free zone at school,
I'm pretty much ready to snuggle under
my duvet and never come out.
Not even the glittery ballet ⟶
pumps Mum surprised me with
when I got home from school
were enough to lift the black

cloud of gloom I had floating over my head. In fact, it wasn't until I slipped Molly's dress on and saw a strange girl reflected back at me in the mirror that I felt the first fluttering of excitement. In ten minutes, Nathan would arrive to pick me up and I'd get to spend the whole evening talking to him. At least I wouldn't have to stress about accidentally ignoring Molly and Shenice – they'd be blanking me on purpose.

The doorbell rang at seven o'clock sharp. Dad got up to answer it but I dived across the room, practically breaking my neck in the process, to stop him from getting there first and unleashing some awful ancient joke (or worse) on an unsuspecting Nathan.

"Hi," I said, as I pulled back the front door to reveal him standing under an umbrella. That's when I realized it was raining, that light, misty sort of drizzle that Shenice hates the most. She claims it turns her hair into frizz faster than sticking her finger in an electric socket, and I suddenly remembered when she'd turned up to my rain-soaked birthday party last year wearing a Sainsbury's bag on her head. Then I forced the memory away, because even if she repeated the look at the ball, I wouldn't be invited to share the joke.

"Hi," Nathan replied, and held out a little square box. "I thought about getting you flowers but I reckoned your dog would probably eat them. So I got you this instead."

With a little gasp of surprise, I opened the box. Nestling inside was a shiny key ring, with a tiny silvery dog attached to it. I smiled, happier than I'd felt in days. "It's gorgeous. Thank you."

"Glad you like it," he said, grinning. "Shall we get going? My mum is waiting in the car."

I peered over his shoulder. His mum waved at me.

"I'm going now," I called and both my parents appeared in the hallway. Dad made me cringe by shaking Nathan's hand and Mum insisted on taking our photo, faffing about with the camera and going on about how fast we were growing up – so EMBARRASSING.

"Dad is picking you and Liam up at ten," she reminded me as I pulled on my coat. "Have a nice time."

"I will," I called and realized I actually meant it.

Maybe it wouldn't be such a bad night after all.

I didn't know who was in charge of turning our dingy school hall into a venue fit for a ball but they'd done an amazing job. Seriously, if I hadn't walked up the school steps and through the double glass doors, I wouldn't have recognized the place where I'd spent many an assembly picking at my nails and daydreaming. The hall had huge

sheets of pastel-coloured satin
sweeping down from the
ceiling, like they have in
swanky wedding venues,
and twisty columns of
balloons in each corner. At one end,
there was a long table covered with
food and drink with helium balloons on
long ribbons, at the other was a stage with
a sparkly silver backdrop behind it and a
huge WOLF BRETHREN banner up above.

"Wow, it looks brilliant," I said, pausing in the
doorway to take it all in.

Nathan smiled. "My mum will be glad you think so,"
he said and, when my forehead crinkled in puzzlement,
went on, "she's on the PTA. They did all the organizing
and decorating for tonight."

That was even more amazing – my mum had trouble organizing enough milk for our breakfasts. Then again, Nathan's mum didn't have Joshua and Ethel keeping her up all night.

It was a whole new experience walking in with Nathan. Seriously, I wouldn't have been surprised if paparazzi had leaped out from behind the drinks table. EVERYONE said hello to him – the boys bumped fists and the girls fluttered their eyelashes. At first I smiled too, expecting people to say hi to me as well. But their eyes kind of slid over me as though I wasn't there and a few actually turned their backs. Once we'd moved on, I had the uncomfortable feeling that people were whispering about me. Nathan was too polite to say anything but I know he noticed. Inside, I was dying. What was going on? Surely this couldn't still be about my hair? Nathan must know about that but he'd never said a word.

Once I'd been ignored by what felt like the entire

lower school, Nathan explained that the plan was for
the band to play for about an hour and then one of the
teachers was going to take over as DJ. I really hoped
it wasn't Mrs Pitt-Rivers – my mental image of her on
the decks, blinged up to the max, wasn't one I wanted
to become a reality. I doubted she'd be down with the
latest tunes, either, and nobody wants to bust a move
to GREENSLEEVES.

And then I saw something that killed off the last
shreds of my good mood entirely. In front of us, a few
girls from our year were whispering, giggling and
pointing. Following the direction of their gaze, I could see
they were looking at Shenice. I wanted to warn her but
she'd flashed me a "don't even think about it" look the
moment she spotted me and Molly had shrugged, so I
wasn't going to risk talking to them.

"Do you want a drink?" Nathan asked, oblivious to
what was going on. "I don't suppose they'll run to a SUGAR

RUSH MOUNTAIN but I can probably get you a Coke."

For a nano-second, I thought about confronting the girls, but it would only make things worse and Shenice wouldn't thank me. Wishing I'd never heard of JUICE ON JUDE'S, or Kelly Anderson, I turned to Nathan and did my best to smile. "Coke would be great, thanks."

It hurts me to say it but WOLF BRETHREN totally smashed it. Anjel fitted in so seamlessly that it felt like she'd always been part of the band, and she definitely looked the part as she strummed her bass. Everyone was rocking and a few Year Nine boys tried to create a mosh pit during "Hunt The Hunter" but the teachers soon broke it up. JOJ had been so certain WOLF BRETHREN were going to split up and it couldn't have been more wrong – it made me wonder how many other friendships Kelly was going to try and ruin with her poisonous pen. ⟶

"They're awesome," Nathan said, nodding at the stage, and I felt a warm rush of sisterly pride. Liam might be a total pain but sometimes I didn't totally hate being related to him.

"Yeah, they're not bad, I suppose."

I glanced sideways, to where Molly and Shenice stood. Molly wore her usual expression of total adoration as she sang along and it didn't look like she even remembered that Anjel had supposedly ruined the band dynamics. Everywhere I looked, people were dancing and singing and even Mrs Pitt-Rivers seemed to be enjoying herself. It reminded me of ST JUDE'S HAS GOT TALENT! when I'd first realized Liam could actually play his guitar. I'd been amazed then at how popular they were, and it seemed like their fan-base had grown, because the cheers and whoops after they'd played their last song went on for ages. And I almost forgot how miserable I was.

"Not bad at all," I said, as Liam and his band mates left the stage. "I wonder who the mystery DJ is."

"Don't look at me," Nathan replied. "I don't know either."

All around us, people were wondering the same thing. The buzz of excitement grew with each passing second. When the hall door opened, every single person turned to look and I wondered if the months of sleeplessness had caught up with me and I'd fallen asleep on my feet, because a nightmare was unfolding right in front of me. The DJ wasn't Mrs Pitt-Rivers at all. It was Mr Ramirez.

I glanced over at Shenice as the whispering started. She was frozen to the spot and looked like she was about to burst into tears. Oblivious, Mr Ramirez walked up to the DJ stand and put an enormous set of headphones over his ears. A minute later, a thumping

195

bassline filled the room and
drowned out the whispers.

Groaning, I put my hands
over my face. "Please tell me this isn't happening."

Nathan looked at me sympathetically and I guessed
he must have heard about what had happened. "Poor
Shenice."

A stab of shame squirmed through me as I wondered
what he'd thought of the eggy photo of me on JOJ, but
my embarrassment was nothing compared to Shenice's.
There was no way I could enjoy myself knowing that she
was so miserable. Each time I looked over, her expression
grew more and more upset. When I spotted a group of
Year Eight boys circling Molly and Shenice, I knew
straight away they were trouble.

Pulling silently on Nathan's sleeve, I edged closer.

"Does your dad do requests?" I heard one jeer loudly and they all cackled with laughter. Shenice's face turned a sullen red and Molly clenched her fists. I'd seen that look before – any minute now, she'd go all HULK SMASH on them and there'd be no going back. I stepped forward. "Leave her alone!"

The boys turned and stared at me.

"Shut it, Humpty," one sneered.

"Don't start anything with her," another said. "She'll put you on JOJ."

That didn't even make sense but I didn't have time to think about it. "I'll tell Mrs Pitt-Rivers."

"Oooh," one mocked, clasping his hands to his face as though he was terrified. "Please don't tell on me!"

Nathan had clearly heard enough, because he stepped in front of me. "Leave it, George," he said.

The boys looked up. "Yeah but—"

Nathan's tone was light but it had a cold edge to it. "I said, leave it."

For a moment I thought they'd argue, but then they sloped off. I opened my mouth to speak but Shenice silenced me with a glare.

"Don't bother," was all she said and, without a word, she and Molly stalked off.

I watched them go. Then I realized someone else was glaring at me. Hannah was standing to one side, and she looked like she hated my guts.

"Someone else you burned, right, Cassidy?" she

sneered, with a hollow laugh. "With friends like you, who needs enemies?"

Firing a final filthy look my way, she disappeared back into the crowd and I realized I was suddenly the centre of attention. People were watching me, whispering, and from the looks on their faces, they weren't being kind. Feeling my cheeks flame, I shut my eyes, willing the universe to send an extremely localized meteor to vaporize me from the planet.

When that failed to materialize, I blinked and saw Nathan watching me. "What did they mean, Cassie?" he asked quietly. "Why did they say you'd put them on JUICE ON JUDE'S?"

And that's when the horrible truth dawned on me. The reason no one wanted to speak to me was because they all thought I was the person behind JOJ. They had no idea it was Kelly – they thought it was ME who'd started the nasty rumours and spilled their secrets. But I couldn't explain any of that – who would believe it was super-nice Kelly, anyway? My lower lip began to tremble. "It's not what you think."

He shook his head, a disgusted expression on his face. "It's you, isn't it? You write JUICE ON JUDE'S."

The room started to spin as I fought back tears. Everywhere I looked, I saw furious faces. It was all too much.

"I think I'm going to be sick," I croaked.

CHAPTER FIFTEEN

Mum didn't ask why I was back so early, or where Liam was. She took one look at my tear-stained face, as Dad shepherded me in from the car, and took me straight upstairs to my room, where I threw myself onto my bed and howled my heart out. Sitting silently beside me, she stroked my hair until I stopped crying.

"Do you want to talk about it?" she asked, offering me a mug of hot chocolate.

Rolo reached up and licked my hand, like he was trying to make me feel better. I rubbed his head absently and shook my head at Mum. The last thing I wanted was to relive the whole horrible evening. And now on top of feeling rubbish about Hannah and Shenice, Nathan thought I was a gossiping bully. It didn't matter how much I denied it, I could tell he thought I was too cowardly to come clean about what had really happened. All I wanted to do was go to sleep and wake up to find it had all been a dream.

I sipped the hot chocolate, letting the rich milky sweetness soothe my frazzled nerves. Those Hogwarts professors are so right about chocolate – it really does have magical properties. But it was going to take more than hot chocolate to make everything better for me. I'd been so stupid. If only I'd kept Hannah's secret to myself then Shenice would never have accused me of betraying her and maybe the whole school wouldn't think I was responsible for JOJ and – and – it made my brain hurt just thinking about it. I pushed the whole tangled mess away and closed my sore, swollen eyes.

"I think I threw up on Nathan's shoes," I sniffed, after a little while.

To her credit, Mum didn't look remotely amused. "I'm sure he understands."

And he thinks I'm evil and nasty, I wanted to add but didn't. Instead, I let out a long, miserable sigh. "There's no coming back from tonight. I don't think he'll ever forgive me."

"He seems like a nice boy," she said, in the same tone she used when she was shushing the babies back to sleep. "I'm sure he'll come round in time."

I wished I could believe her but the truth was I didn't think Nathan would ever be able to look at me again, never mind speak to me. And no one would believe Kelly was behind JOJ, there was no point in even trying to tell the truth. It didn't matter that I'd been a victim too – everyone probably thought I'd posted the Egghead story myself to cover my tracks. The way things were going, I'd be a complete social outcast by the time the half-term holiday arrived.

My head felt hot and aching. "I think I might go to sleep now," I said, and hesitated, scared that the horrible empty feeling would come back the moment I was on my own. It was like I was four years old again and afraid of the dark. "I – will you stay with me until I'm asleep?"

She smiled. "Of course. Why don't you get ready for bed while I go and check on the twins?"

Once she was gone, I got into my pyjamas and hung Molly's dress on the back of my door. Then I slipped into

the bathroom to throw some cold water on my face.
My reflection stared back at me from the mirror as I
brushed my teeth, all puffy eyes and blotchy cheeks.
I looked away and finished as fast as I could.

Mum was waiting when I got back to my room.

"Sweet dreams," she said, as I wriggled under the
duvet. "It'll all seem better in the morning."

I nodded and laid my cheek against the cool cotton
of my pillow. Rolo jumped up and curled up beside my
feet. "Sorry for being such a baby," I mumbled. "That's
the last thing you need."

She leaned down and kissed my forehead. "Don't
be silly," she murmured softly. "You'll always be a baby
to me."

I am starting to wonder if my mother IS secretly a witch. Firstly, she conjured up a mug of hot chocolate exactly when I needed one and then she cast some kind of magic spell on me because not only did I sleep for the whole night without waking up once, but her prediction that everything would seem clearer in the morning was right too. At the very least, she has been watching too much Derren Brown and did some weird hypnotism thing on me.

I lay in bed for ages, thinking things through. There is no getting away from the fact that I vommed on Nathan's feet, and Shenice and Hannah think I totally ruined their lives, and the rest of the school thinks I pretended to wash my hair in a frying pan. What I need is a way to put everything back to how it was a month ago but, short of getting my hands on a time machine, I can't see what I can do to turn the clock back. It would be easier to start my life again under an assumed name.

When I did go downstairs, Mum wasn't impressed by my plan.

"Changing schools isn't the answer," she said firmly, as she changed Ethel's nappy. "You'd be better off facing up to whatever the issue is. Can Liam help you sort it out?"

I stared at her, bouncing Joshua on my knee and wondering how to break it to her that her first born wasn't in the running for Big Brother of the Year.

"Not unless he's discovered the secret of time travel," I said.

"Here," she said, handing me Ethel's used nappy in a little peach-coloured sack. Wrinkling my nose, I wrapped my arms around Joshua and tied a knot in the bag. They don't tell you about the pure evilness that comes out of babies' bottoms when you learn about reproduction at school. If they did, the human race would be doomed.

Mum sat back and looked at me. "I think it's about time you told me what's been going on, don't you?"

And just like that, I did.

When I'd finished, she pressed her lips together the way she does when she's trying not to explode. Nervously, I eyed Ethel gurgling merrily in her arms – surely she couldn't lose it with a baby on her lap?

"Are you really angry?" I ventured, after a while.

Her eyes flashed. "Not with you. I'm angry with this Kelly girl for being a nasty piece of work. I'm angry that the school aren't aware that it's happening." She let out a long, slow breath. "And I'm angry with Liam – he should have told someone what was going on."

And that's when my heart started thudding so fast that I thought I might have a heart attack. "Don't have a go at Liam," I begged, picturing what he'd do to me if he got into trouble over this. "He hates it just as much as I do, especially since **WOLF BRETHREN** was on **JOJ** so much."

Mum shook her head. "That's the problem, Cassie. He's old enough to know what to do in situations like this. Bullying is bullying."

"He's going to kill me," I said in a dull voice. "I won't need to change schools. I'll already be dead."

"Don't be silly, of course he won't. And you're not going to change schools," Mum said briskly. "Deep down, I think you already know what you have to do."

The really depressing thing was, she was right. I was

the one who'd worked out that Kelly was masterminding JUICE ON JUDE'S, which meant I was the one who'd have to report her, even if it did mean owning up to my part in the whole mess. Bleakly, I nodded. "I'll speak to Mr Bearman on Monday."

"Good girl," she said, patting my knee. "You know it makes sense."

She got up and carried Ethel into the kitchen, leaving me reeling in unhappy silence.

"Learn from my mistakes," I whispered into Joshua's fuzzy head. "Never trust Mum with anything."

Seriously, I'm not sure I even know what just happened. One minute we were discussing the possibility of changing schools and the next I was spilling my guts.

I'm telling you, Derren Brown could learn a lot from her.

Last Will and Testament of Cassidy Bond

Just in case I do not survive Monday...

I, Cassidy Bond, being of sound body and mind (or as sound as it can be under the circumstances) do bequeath all my worldly goods as follows:

To Mum and Dad, I leave the £24.75 in my Post Office savings account. Spend it wisely.

To Molly and Shenice, I leave my Superdry sweatshirt and my Jelly Belly jelly bean dispenser, plus my Droids poster and music collection.

To Joshua and Ethel, I bequeath my bedroom. Don't let Rolo sleep on the bed, he bites your toes while you sleep.

And to Rolo, I leave my Fluffy Bunny cuddly toy with the half-chewed ears – finish him off with my blessing, boy.

Liam, I know you would like my new camera so I have hidden it somewhere you will never find it. Serves you right for being the worst brother ever.

That concludes my last will and testament.

Cassidy Bond

E-PETITION
Number of signatures: 1458

CHAPTER SIXTEEN

It is done. First thing this morning, I went to see
Mr Bearman and even though I felt like the biggest
grass in the history of grasses (and I don't mean the
wavy, green stuff), I told him everything.

He listened without saying much, then thanked
me for telling him and asked me to leave it with him.
I overheard someone say that ten minutes after I spoke
to Mr Bearman, the entire press gang except me was
sitting outside the Headteacher's office and then he and

Mrs Pitt-Rivers called them in one by one to do Good Cop, Bad Cop with them. Apparently Mel, Kieran and Toby were sent back to class pretty quickly, because it became totally obvious they weren't involved. The rest of them were sitting on the seats of shame for most of the morning. Meggie Defoe swears she heard screaming when she was monitoring the late book but I think she made that bit up. Anyway, their parents have been called into school, the website has vanished and someone said that Kelly might go to court but I think that's probably an exaggeration.

The other thing is that **HEY JUDE'S!** has been closed until further notice, which I'm kind of sad about as I never actually got anything published. Then again, I didn't even finish my Year Seven Outward Bound article so maybe I'm not cut out for journalism after all – I'm fairly sure it shouldn't be as hard as I found it. And I paid a pretty high price for my time in the press gang – Shenice still isn't talking to me and I avoided looking at

Nathan in registration. I suppose he knows who the real Juicers are by now but I'm too embarrassed to talk to him — I did vom on his shoes, after all. The news of my innocence will reach him eventually, I guess.

Call me stupid but after speaking to Mr Bearman, I didn't think about what Kelly might do afterwards. I was so relieved to get the weight of the website off my shoulders that for a blissful few hours I thought I might be able to put it all behind me. But when I saw Kelly waiting by the school gates at the end of the day, her two gum-snapping mates beside her, I knew I was in deep, deep trouble.

It was too late to run — she'd seen me. A cruel smile crossed her face as she nudged her friends. Frantically, I looked around for backup — Liam, Molly or even Nathan — but although I was surrounded by people, no one was meeting my eye and I knew I couldn't count on any of them for help. Most of them suspected I'd been involved in JUICE ON JUDE'S somehow and it was going to take time to set them straight. Quaking in my navy blue ballet pumps, I trudged towards the gate and prepared myself for the worst.

"Look who we have here," Kelly sneered as I got closer. "It's Judas Bond."

A wide circle cleared around me, as though everyone knew what was coming and no one wanted to be caught up in it. I started to wish I'd gone for the swapping schools option after all.

"I'm not scared of you, Kelly," I called, and my voice only wobbled a little bit.

Kelly bared her teeth. "You should be. I got in a lot of trouble because of you."

I drew level with her and screwed up as much

courage as I could. If I had to go down, I'd go down fighting, or at least scratching.

"No, you got in a lot of trouble because you wrote horrible things about people who couldn't answer back," I said, and all the misery of the last few days turned suddenly into furious rage. My hands balled into fists. "You're nothing but a coward, hiding behind a computer screen and thinking you're someone important because you know how to twist the truth. Well, here's some breaking news, Kelly – no one likes a big fat liar."

Kelly's mouth dropped open in shock and a flicker of uncertainty crossed her face. I guessed she'd expected me to roll over and beg for mercy but I was way too angry for that.

We'd attracted a big audience now and they watched in uneasy silence as we squared up to each other.

Kelly stepped forward and stuck her face up close to mine. "It's three against one, Cassie," she said, in a low, menacing tone. "We're going to make you pay."

"Leave her alone!"

The shout rang out from the back of the crowd. I looked up to see Molly pushing her way through, her face twisted with anger. Shenice was right behind her, panting as though she'd just run the cross-country course. My heart leaped with happiness as they came to stand next to me, and we glared at Kelly together.

She looked them up and down and laughed. "I'm supposed to be scared of three Year Seven brats, am I?"

I couldn't help it — fear forced its way through the

cracks in my bravado. They were Year Tens and much bigger than us.

I didn't even know Nathan was there until he joined us. "Make that four."

The breath caught in my throat — did that mean he DIDN'T hate me after all?

Kelly let out a cruel-sounding cackle. "Oh, please. I can easily turn your life at St Jude's into a living hell, Cassidy. And none of your little friends can stop me."

There was a rustling in the crowd and a voice called out, "How about a group of Year Tens, Kelly?"

Liam stepped forwards, the rest of WOLF BRETHREN behind him, and a wave of absolute relief washed over me. I couldn't wait to see Kelly try to stand up to THEM.

"Get lost, Liam. She's a dirty little sneak who needs to be taught a lesson," Kelly spat.

Liam glanced at me briefly and I tried not to cringe – it looked like he'd have plenty to say to me later. But right now, he had my back. "Yeah, but the thing is, she's MY dirty little sneak," he said, standing protectively in front of me. "So if you want to teach her a lesson, you'll have to go through us first, okay?"

The mood of the crowd had shifted. WOLF BRETHREN were the closest thing St Jude's had to rock stars and they had a lot of fans. And now that Kelly had made it clear she wasn't PRINCESS PERFECT after all and I wasn't the one who'd been behind JOJ, the tide of opinion seemed to be turning my way. A long silence crackled as Kelly weighed up her options. Then she wheeled abruptly away.

"Losers!" she called over her shoulder.

The word broke the spell and everyone started to talk at once. As the crowd started to thin, Liam turned to me.

"I'll see you at home," he growled, before I could thank him, and sloped off down the road.

Puffing out a shaky breath, I glanced at Molly and Shenice. "Thanks for trying to help."

Molly smiled. "I thought we were dead. Until our knight in shining armour turned up."

WHICH ONE? I wondered, turning to thank Nathan, but he'd vanished. And who was I trying to kid? Molly had meant Liam and this time, I couldn't argue.

"Nah, we had her running scared long before he showed up," Shenice said, and we all laughed.

We ambled slowly down the road.

"Look, I'm sorry about your mum and Mr Ramirez," I burst out. "It really wasn't me who told Kelly."

Shenice's cheeks went a bit pink. "Yeah, I know. I found out this morning that Jimmy Nelson overheard me talking to you about it in the playground and told Kelly everything." She squinted at me. "Sorry I accused you."

I couldn't really blame her for putting two and two together and coming up with me – I'd have probably done exactly the same in her shoes. And the truth was, I had dropped Hannah in it – I owed her a huge apology. "It's okay. Does your mum know her secret is out?"

She nodded and looked even more embarrassed. "Yeah, that's the other thing. It turns out Mum ISN'T dating Mr Ramirez at all. She's booked this big surprise holiday to Spain for the summer and he's been giving her Spanish lessons."

I stopped walking, my eyes wide. "Shut up! So he's not going to be your stepdad?"

Grinning, she shook her head. "Nope."

Linking my arms through hers and Molly's, I let out a deep groan. "We're complete idiots, aren't we?"

"Speak for yourself," Molly objected. Her gaze slid sideways. "Nice of Nathan to stand up for you. I think he feels bad for the way he treated you."

Now that my problems with Kelly were out of the way, I had two bits of unfinished business. Making it up to Hannah was one, getting over my embarrassment with Nathan was the other.

I pursed my lips thoughtfully.

"Any idea what Riverside Secondary School is like?"

CHAPTER SEVENTEEN

Things are starting to settle down again at Bond HQ.
I'd really missed hanging out with Molly and Shenice.
Even though we only fell out for a few days, it felt like
the world had ended and it was great to be giggling
and chatting with them again. Liam tried to have a go
at me for exposing the truth about JOJ but his heart
wasn't really in it and I decided that he was secretly
pleased it was gone. I'm just guessing here but it MIGHT
have something to do with Anjel stopping me after their
WOLF BRETHREN rehearsal on Wednesday night and

congratulating me for standing up to the bullies. I really like her. Hope they don't get together – aside from the fact that Molly would be totally devastated, Anjel is **WAY** too good for Liam. All I need now is to learn how to do **MEMORY CHARMS** so that I can erase Nathan's memory of me redecorating his shoes and life will be back to normal.

Mr Bearman stopped me after English today and asked me if I'd had any trouble as a result of coming clean. I thought about telling him what had happened after school on Monday but Kelly had stayed out of my way since and I reckoned she'd leave me alone from now on.

"Not really, sir."

"Good," he said. "Let me know if Kelly bothers you. You did a really brave thing by blowing the whistle."

It didn't feel brave at the time – it felt like I was

doomed. But I didn't say that. "Thanks, sir."

"HEY JUDE'S! is restarting after the half-term holiday, with a brand-new editor and a strict code of practice," he said, looking at me enquiringly. "Mel and Kieran are staying on. I hope you'll continue as our Year Seven Correspondent?"

I thought about it for a few seconds. Being a reporter had seemed like fun at the beginning but I'd seen a nasty side to the job that I didn't really like. I didn't seem to have much of a nose for a story, either. "Probably not, sir. I don't think journalism is my Thing after all."

He sighed. "Well, if you change your mind, you know where I am."

And that was it – my chance at the Golden Nib Award was gone.

Never mind, plenty of other awards in the sea...
I wonder how hard it is to win the Nobel Peace Prize?

Saying sorry to Hannah was one of the hardest things
I've ever done. She wasn't exactly warm when I tracked
her down in the playground, but at least she listened. And
when I'd finished grovelling and explaining and grovelling
some more, she stared at me for the longest time before
she spoke.

"Just don't do it again, okay?"

I nodded as hard as I could and she almost smiled as
she walked away. Heaving a sigh of relief, I went to find
Molly and Shenice. I've definitely
learned my lesson – the only juice
I'll be sharing from now on is
the kind you get from oranges. ➔

We'd got to the final lesson of the day when I was summoned to Mrs Pitt-Rivers's office. The idiots on the back tables let out a low rumble, as though I was in trouble for something. Outwardly I ignored them, but inside I was worried. What if Kelly had found a way to blame me for something on JUICE ON JUDE'S? What if Mrs Pitt-Rivers had the phone in her hand right this minute, poised to call my mum?

"Ah, Cassidy," she said when I poked my head around the door to her office. "Come in and sit down, please."

I did as I was told, scrutinizing her face for a clue that I was about to be hauled over the coals. There wasn't one – she looked as grumpy as she always did.

"I've been asked to talk to you about your petition," she said, folding her hands on the huge wooden desk in front of her.

I blinked. The petition? I'd almost forgotten about that. It felt like a lifetime ago that I'd started it and such a lot had happened. Come to think of it, wasn't it that petition that had got me noticed by Kelly in the first place? And now it looked like Mrs Pitt-Rivers had found out about it. Great.

"Okay," I replied, preparing for a telling-off.

She stared at me for a moment, then sighed. "While it's hardly a matter of national importance, it appears that the Governors have heard your rallying cry. Having reviewed the school uniform policy, they've decided to amend it. After the half-term break, girls may wear trousers to school if they choose."

BOOM! It was like an earthquake had hit my central nervous system. I shook my head to clear it, certain I must have misheard. Had she really just said that the Governors had listened to our views? And that something

I'd done had actually made a difference?
I sat back in the seat, stunned.

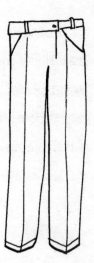

"Wow," I said faintly. "Really?"

Her lips thinned. "Yes, really."

"Wow," I said again. "Thanks, miss."

She stared at me for a few more seconds, then shuffled some papers around on her desk. "It seems you've made quite an impact since you joined St Jude's, Cassidy." Her eyes crinkled into the merest hint of a smile. "I do like people who stand up for what they believe in. Well done."

I got up, wondering if there were any more aftershocks waiting to hit me. Had Mrs Pitt-Rivers just given me a compliment? Or was I totally deluding myself?

"Thanks," I said and tottered back to my lesson. As I walked, the full impact of what I'd achieved hit me. My petition might not have reached the hallowed doors of Westminster but it had definitely done its job. We'd taken on the establishment and we had won!

I can't wait to come back after the half-term holidays. Never mind that a mini-heatwave is forecast for the beginning of June and temperatures are set to soar – trousers are the new black and I'm going to make sure every single girl wears them!

To: <u>BondGirl007</u>

From: <u>LittleBittyKitty</u>

Hi Cassie,

I hope you don't mind me messaging you – I got your email address from Nathan Crossfield. Anyway, I just wanted to say that you rock! Nathan sent me a link to your petition (I signed!) and it made me think about the uniform rules at my school. So I have started my own petition, based on yours. It's early days but it has over five hundred signatures already and I am sure it will persuade our Headteacher to let girls wear trousers if they want.

I would never have thought of this if you hadn't done it first. Cassidy Bond, you are TOTALLY my hero!

Luv

GIRL POWER!

Chelsea xx

CHAPTER EIGHTEEN

There's something magical about the last day before half-term. The teachers are too tired to set much work, the kids are too busy making plans to concentrate on much and everyone has one eye on the clock. Since I was pretty sure the whole MAY BALL / JOJ thing had put Nathan off me for life, I'd given up hope that we'd ever share a SUGAR RUSH MOUNTAIN MOMENT again and I couldn't wait for the holidays to start. Even a week with Mum and the twins was better than another week of being ignored. She'd promised to take us out for the day, although knowing my luck it would be somewhere like Baby Yoga.

Anyway, by the time the bell finally rang at the end of the day, I couldn't get out of the door fast enough. As Molly, Shenice and I walked down the road, a sense of peace descended on me. One whole week in which the biggest drama would be where Rolo had hidden my shoes.

"Are we doing anything next week?" Shenice asked.

I shrugged. "You can come over to mine for a sleepover, if you want."

Molly shook her head so hard her curls bounced out of their ponytail. "What, and stay awake all night listening to the twins? No, thanks."

I smiled. "It's okay, they sleep through the night now."

She let out a heavy sigh. "Really? But now where am I supposed to go when the zombie apocalypse happens?"

Shenice dug into her bag and pulled out a brightly coloured flyer. "Speaking of places to go, my mum gave me this last night."

She held it out and Molly and I stopped walking to study it.

"ETON DORNEY DANCE AND DRAMA ACADEMY," I read. "UNLEASH YOUR INNER SUPERSTAR?"

"It's not on until the summer holidays but Mum says it's being run by a friend of hers who used to be on in the West End," Shenice explained. "I think it might be a laugh. Fancy it?"

I thought about our family summer holiday to Happy Sands – a drama school might be exactly what I need to take my mind of the fact that I will probably be an OAP before I get to meet Mickey Mouse. I gazed down at the flyer, imagining myself standing on a stage with an adoring audience staring up at me. A buzz of excitement hit me – what if ACTING was my THING?

"What do you think?" I asked Molly, knowing long before I saw the enthusiasm in her eyes that she'd be up for it. Molly is an amazing singer – she's going to be a real star one day.

"Are you kidding?" she said. "Let's do it!"

We wandered along, planning what we'd be best at. Then my phone pinged. I pulled it out of my pocket, saw Nathan's name and shoved it quickly away again, before the others could see the screen.

"Who was that from?" Molly demanded, grabbing my hand and yanking my phone back out. "I knew it!"

She held it out and showed Shenice.

"It's from HIM," Shenice breathed, her eyes wide. "Aren't you going to read it?"

I shook my head. "No. I've decided I'm done beating myself up over something I can't change."

"Oh, for goodness' sake! The two of you need your heads banging together," Molly said, and she snatched the phone out of my hand. Her face didn't change as she read the message and carried on walking as though nothing had happened.

And now I was torn. On the one hand, I didn't want to know what the message said, but on the other, the suspense of not knowing was killing me. "Well?"

"Well what?" she asked. "I thought you were done."

I counted to ten. "I am but now that you've read it, I want to know what it says."

She lifted the phone and opened up the message. "It says, *Hey Cassie, Want to climb Sugar Rush Mountain again sometime?*"

"It does not!" I squealed, feeling my skin turn bright red, all the way up to my hair. "Oh Em Gee, it does not."

Molly grinned and showed Shenice. "It does."

"Looks like he still likes you," Shenice said in a sing-song voice.

YES! I totally cannot believe it – Nathan Crossfield, the COOLEST boy in the school, is not completely revolted by me. Better still, he wants to share a milkshake with me! Do not tell Mum I said this but MAYBE she was right about sticking things out at St Jude's, especially now I've exposed Kelly and struck a blow for women's rights – at least where our legs are concerned. It gives me a lovely warm feeling to know that when Ethel is old enough to start St Jude's, she'll be allowed to do it in trousers. I reckon that Che Guevara dude would approve.

Journalism might not be my Thing but I've definitely learned a trick or two. Now bring on that Sugar Rush!

The End